THE ORPHAN AND THE COACHMAN

Amelia Smarts

D1707368

Published by Amelia Smarts
ameliasmarts.com

Smarts, Amelia
The Orphan and the Coachman

Cover Design by designrans
Images by Period Images

This book is intended for adults only. Spanking
and other sexual activities represented in this
book are fantasies only, intended for adults.

CHAPTER ONE

Missouri, 1871

Callie lay on the floor of the closet, her knees pulled up to her chest. Her eyes were shut tight, but she would have had the same view with them open. Not a drop of light could be seen in the small space, which was located in the belly of the house in a room without windows. She didn't know if it was night or day.

To keep her company were roaches, which didn't scare her as much as the rats that sometimes occupied the space. Still, she could hear the rodents scratching behind the wall, a constant reminder that they might join her at any moment. The stench in the closet was something Callie never smelled anywhere else—to her, it was best described as fear, but it was likely derived from a cocktail of dirty clothes, rat droppings, and rotten wood.

"This is the last time that cock-sucking sozzle will ever lock me in here," she said out loud.

It felt good to say the words, though she wasn't entirely sure what they meant. She'd overheard the phrase from a man exiting the saloon, and it sounded vulgar enough to describe Mrs. Bentley, her worst enemy.

It was Callie's eighteenth birthday. Well, either that or her birthday had already passed, depending on how long she'd been in the closet. Time in there felt immeasurable, infinite, slow. The exact day didn't really matter, since no one had ever celebrated it and she certainly didn't see it as anything special. However, this birthday was important because it marked her official adulthood, the day she would no longer be a ward of the state. She'd been counting down the minutes, waiting for the time when she'd be permitted to escape from the orphans' home, but she hadn't escaped one last punishment.

A wave of terror washed over her. What if Bentley had left her to die, wishing for her to experience the ultimate punishment? Callie contained her panic by humming. She told herself that was irrational. Bentley wouldn't murder her; it would be too much trouble. When Callie grew weary of humming, she counted out loud to one thousand, using the pulse she felt at her neck as a metronome. Then she started at zero again.

Mrs. Bentley released her eventually. By the time she did, Callie's tongue was swollen from thirst and her throat burned. She was so hungry that her limbs shook and she struggled to walk.

She didn't know how long she'd been locked away. Maybe only a day, though it felt like much longer. With labored steps, she trudged to the well on the far side of the property. She dunked her cupped hands in the bucket and drank the cool water until her throat no longer burned. She couldn't remember water ever tasting so sweet, though surely it had tasted just as good the last time she'd been parched after hours in the closet.

Out of concern for Callie's safety, a well-meaning citizen had reported to Mrs. Bentley that he'd spotted Callie wandering the town again after dark. Bentley didn't care about the children's safety, only that it made her look incompetent and forced her to defend how she ran the orphans' home to the townsfolk. Mrs. Bentley would punish any child who inconvenienced or embarrassed her. Callie did her best to avoid doing either, but her very presence bothered the woman.

For more than a decade, Callie had suffered this terrible punishment time and time again. She'd first been relegated to the closet only a couple of days after she was placed in the home following her ma's death of consumption, for a small infraction Callie couldn't recall. Her terror over that first punishment led to an extreme fear of the dark, which caused her to scream in the night and resulted in Mrs. Bentley throwing her in the closet to drown out the noise, creating a vicious cycle of fear she couldn't escape. Each time she suffered a stint in the closet, she felt just as terrified as the previous time. Often, Mrs. Bentley would forget to let her out in the morning, so her time locked away was sometimes longer than would be considered reasonable even by Bentley's cruel standards.

Her thirst quenched, Callie left the home for good and didn't look back. She needed to find food, and fast. As she walked the mile to the town of St. Louis by the light of the moon, she placed her hand inside the small suede pouch she always kept strapped to her hip. She felt her cameo brooch, the only thing she still owned of her ma's. Brushing her fingers along the ridges of the etched profile brought her a sense of peace. She shifted her hand and strummed the edges of the six precious letters from her future husband, Albert, who promised her a happy life as a mail-order bride. Tucked into the letters was the stagecoach ticket for her trip west that Albert had paid for. She knew the ticket displayed a departure date two weeks in the future, but she would try to get on an earlier stagecoach. She needed a new life, and she needed it now.

Her planning was interrupted by the gnawing in her stomach. *One thing at a time*, she told herself. She made her way to the place she'd gone before for a meal in the middle of the night —the saloon—because it was the only business still open at that late hour. As she approached the bar, the raucous sound of drunk men singing along with a piano reached her ears. Her spirits lifted considerably after a few more steps, for there outside the saloon, leaning against the wall with a bottle of whiskey in his hand, was Sam. He smiled drunkenly at her through watery eyes.

"Well, if it isn't the wandering angelica," he drawled.

Callie offered him a weak smile in return. "Hi, Sam. How you doing today?"

"Fair to middlin'. The wife's pregnant with baby number seven and as mad as an old wet hen about it. Blames it on me, of course. You wouldn't wanna be around my missus right now." He let out a low whistle and shook his head.

If Callie weren't so hungry, she might have been amused. Sam often complained about his wife, but Callie had seen the two of them together, and Sam doted on her and looked at her like she hung the moon and stars in the sky. He loved each and every one of his six children too, and he would love the seventh just as much. Callie's heart often ached and burned with jealousy that she wasn't one of his kids.

"I know it's a lot to ask, Sam, especially with you having another nipper on the way, but I'm wondering if you might buy me a meal. I'm awful hungry."

"Sure, darlin'," he said, without a moment's hesitation. His face twisted into a scowl. "The old harpy lock you in the closet again?"

She bit her lip and nodded. With an angry grunt, he handed her his whiskey bottle. "Hold that and I'll go fetch you somethin'. No more than one swig, though, ya hear? I'll tan your hide if you drink more. That's my sanity and I need lots of it, believe you me."

Callie smiled and nodded at him, and then watched him disappear inside the saloon. She wouldn't drink his whiskey, but she knew that even if she did, he wouldn't punish her. He had a loose tongue and a soft heart.

Callie was the same age as Sam's eldest daughter. Years ago he had tried to convince his wife to take her in after finding out how badly she was treated at the orphans' home. His wife refused, though, saying he could barely afford to feed his own family off his cowhand salary and she wasn't about to let another child into the fold. Still, Callie had been able to count on the kindhearted cowboy over the years to buy her a square meal every so often from his limited income.

It was through Sam that Callie had become acquainted with her fiancé. In St. Louis, there were more women than men, but Sam told her that out west, men outnumbered women six to one and were looking for mail-order brides. Shortly after she turned seventeen, he showed her an advertisement in the paper.

Lonesome miner has struck it rich, wants wife to share stake and prospects. Should be of sound mind and good character. Respond to Albert Smith in Sacramento, California.

Callie had responded, which had begun a series of letters between them. The only thing Callie looked forward to, and with great hope for happiness, was her future marriage to Albert. She imagined that he was very rich and very kind. He would murmur sweet, romantic words in her ear and take her to his bed to do all the wicked things that unmarried women weren't supposed to think about but which Callie pondered quite often.

Of course, Albert didn't know anything real about her. She'd never written about growing up in an orphans' home. As far as he knew, she was a well-bred shopkeeper's daughter who possessed the manners and charm of a lady. She'd sprinkled her letters with words such as 'culture' and 'colloquial' that she'd read in books found in the home's attic, and she'd reported her frequent attendance at operas and theater, with colorful descriptions of the actors and props that were half born of her imagination and half copied out of the dusty books.

Sam returned with a piping-hot plate of food and handed it to her as she handed back his bottle of whiskey. Callie could have wept. On the plate were two large potatoes, a generous cut of steak, and a biscuit slathered with butter and honey.

"Thank you ever so much, Sam. I know this must've cost a fortune."

"You're worth it, Callie." In a rare moment

of sobered speech, he said, "Don't let anyone make you think you're not, just 'cuz of how you grew up. Here, take the change." He slipped into her hand a quarter and a penny. "That penny is lucky," he said, giving her a wink. "Best keep it with you, not spend it."

She took refuge for the night behind the tack in the town's livery, making sure to stay out of sight. The summer air ensured that she kept warm overnight. With a lump of hay for a pillow, Callie fell asleep humming and dreaming of a better life —one that included a husband, a home to call her own, and closets without locks.

❊ ❊ ❊

Jude downed his shot of whiskey in one gulp and flicked a nickel on the bar as a tip. It spun and settled on the flat surface as the heat from the liquor settled in his belly. "A little bottled courage is better than coffee in the morning, I always say. Until next time, Dobbin."

The barkeep scraped the nickel across the bar to the edge and caught it in his hand, then shoved it in his pocket. "I tend to agree with you there. Have a good journey and be safe. I hear bandits have been robbing stagecoaches at the Texas–New Mexico border."

"Yeah, that's old news." Jude stood from his stool. He patted his Colt revolver on his left hip. Jude was right-handed, but his other hip contained his more oft-used weapon, a horsewhip coiled in a ring that fell to his knee. "It's better to have a shotgun rider up front in the box with me, but Abe's missus is sick so he can't come along. As my army buddies were quick to point out, my aim's not even as good as the worst gunslinger's, but it'll have to do this go-around."

Dobbin shook his head. He picked up a white bar towel and wiped the wet ring left over from Jude's whiskey tumbler. "You'd think Wells Fargo would give drivers more of a backup plan. It ain't good business, making whips like you responsible for leading the team *and* guarding the passengers."

Placing his black Stetson on his head, Jude grinned. "I'll be sure to let Mr. Wells know you said so, my friend. Anyway, I'd better make hay while the sun still shines. You take care now."

The men said their goodbyes, and Jude strode out the double swinging doors into the warm summer air. In the street stood his stagecoach, right on time and ready to go. The groom was performing a last-minute check of Stormy's hooves for debris. Stormy, one of the leaders of the four-horse outfit, was the smallest, smartest, and most alert horse. Her counterpart was Thunder, also one of the smaller and smarter horses. The two in the rear were large, powerful, and dumb as a box of rocks. It was a good team that Jude used most every time in the first leg. The horses would pull the stagecoach for a hundred miles, until they reached a swing station, where they would be traded out for a new team. The same would happen twenty times after that, until he and his passengers reached their destination in Sacramento.

Even after having driven a coach for nearly five years, Jude still felt apprehensive at the beginning of each new trip. It was a dangerous profession, one he thought he'd be done with by the time he reached age thirty, but his thirtieth birthday had come and gone, and another year was upon him. Both occupations of Jude's adult life were dangerous, first as a soldier in the Civil War and then as a whip for Wells Fargo.

He longed for the more peaceful existence of his youth, when he followed his pa around on his sprawling ranch, learning all there was to know about raising horses and cows. He recalled learning to ride when he was barely knee-high to his pa, and never far from his mind was the hope that someday he would own a ranch of his own. His dreams of a different life included a pretty wife with a sweet disposition, who would bake him cherry pies and keep his bed warm at night. Jude would have stopped driving if he'd met such a woman to settle down with, but no such woman existed in Jude's life, and he reckoned he might as well continue to earn a lucrative living while he was unattached.

His four passengers loitered around the coach and looked up expectantly as he approached.

Jude openly appraised the people he was responsible for safely transporting from St. Louis to Sacramento. They appeared to be two married couples—the most common type of passengers. One couple was smartly dressed and obviously came from money. The woman wore a broad hat that sprouted colorful plumes, and the man wore a silk tie. They held their heads a little higher in the air than their poorer traveling companions. There was a soft look about the rich folks, and Jude guessed that they would be whining about the discomfort of traveling after no more than fifty miles.

The man in the silk tie held out his hand. "Tom Tucker, former U.S. senator," he said. "Pleased to meet you."

It wasn't unusual for his passengers to inform him of their political rank or other important stature in society, but everyone knew it meant very little on their journey. During the staging, the driver was king, master, president, or God—whichever sounded most important to a person. The driver could choose one or none of them to sit next to him in the highly sought-after box seat, which didn't shake as badly as the seats in the coach, and the passengers would rely on him to safely transport them across half the country—no easy feat, where Indians, outlaws, bad weather, and poor roads were only some of the potential problems they could face.

Jude gave the former senator's hand a firm

squeeze. "Howdy, Senator. I'm Jude Johnson. I answer to Jude, driver, or whip."

The other man introduced himself. "I'm Billy Adams and I'm headed west to work on the tracks. The railroad augers are lookin' for blacksmiths like me and I hear tell that they're paying a pretty penny for our services."

Jude noticed a shotgun strapped to Billy's back, something that provided him with relief. If they ran into trouble, Jude wouldn't be the only one with a gun.

"This here is my wife," Billy continued. He placed a hand on his wife's shoulder and gave it a gentle squeeze.

"You can call me Annie." She smiled at Jude politely when he tipped his hat. She had a sturdy look to her, with tanned skin and red hands, likely from scrubbing dishes and clothes, but her eyes were soft and kind.

Jude tipped his Stetson at the senator's wife too, who introduced herself as Mrs. Tucker as she rearranged her cumbersome hat using delicate white hands with manicured nails. She already looked uncomfortable, and Jude made a silent bet to himself that she would be ridding herself of her hat before they reached the home station in Paselo.

Introductions out of the way, Jude cleared his throat, ready to inform the travelers about some particulars of the journey. He didn't get the chance to speak, however, for at that moment a loud female voice cut through the quiet. "I'm here!" the voice shouted.

Jude turned to find a girl running toward the group. She kicked up dust behind her, and when she stopped in front of Jude, she bent and placed her hands on her knees, breathing hard.

"Sorry I'm late," she panted. "I had to say goodbye to a friend of mine. I reckon I won't be seeing him again." The girl wore a thin yellow dress with holes in the sleeves and tears along the seams of the skirt, revealing an off-white petticoat underneath. Her hair, the same dirty gold color as her dress, fell wildly around her shoulders except where it was pasted to her sweaty brow.

Jude rested a hand on his hip and allowed her a moment to catch her breath before he addressed her. "You've got the wrong coach, miss. I'm only transporting four today. Another stagecoach will travel the line in two weeks. That must be yours."

The girl straightened and shook her head emphatically. "No, sir, this is definitely my coach. I specifically asked for you as the whip. I know your coach has the best reaches."

Jude knew she was referring to the leather strap braces underneath, which gave the coach a swinging motion, unlike the old-fashioned spring suspension, which jostled passengers up and down. The reaches were top-of-the-line, but most people didn't know one type of reach from the other. Jude found it interesting that she did. He frowned thoughtfully and held out his hand, palm up. "Let me see your ticket then."

The girl reached into a suede pouch at her side and pulled out a thick strip of paper, which she placed on his hand with her eyes downcast. Jude studied it carefully. It was a valid ticket, but the original departure date had been scratched off and the current date rewritten in calligraphy —a pitiful attempt to resemble the letters of the station's ink stamp.

He handed it back to her. "That's quite dishonest of you, scratching out the real date. Did you really reckon you'd get away with that?"

The girl stood a little straighter and focused wide green eyes on him that seemed bright against her fair skin. "I promise you won't be sorry if you let me come along. I can take care of the horses. I was a groom for the best stable in Missouri for a year. Also, I know how to repair each and every wagon part on that outfit," she said, pointing at the stagecoach.

Jude opened the door to the body of the coach and held out his hand to assist Annie up the steps. To the girl he said, "I don't need a groom or repairman. They're at every swing and home station along the line. Run on home now, young lady."

"That would be mighty difficult, mister, seeing as how my home is in California. I swear, you won't be sorry if I come. I'm real useful. Have you heard of Nurse Nightingale? She personally taught me how to stitch up wounds and tend to fevers and other sicknesses. Imagine if something happened on the line and you had among your passengers someone with medical training. That would be a right smart benefit, I'd think."

Jude sighed. "Why do I get the feelin' you're stretching the truth a bit?"

She didn't pick up on the rhetorical nature of the question. "I don't know. Maybe you're not a trusting person. But what I say is true. Why, I bet I'd be the most useful person of all your passengers. I can shoot a target from three hundred yards away and hit it ninety-nine out of a hundred times. If you need a guard, I'm your huckleberry," she asserted, jutting a thumb at her chest.

Jude groaned and rolled his eyes. Reaching down, he picked up the senator's large red travel case and hefted it onto the back of the coach. He secured it to the boot with straps. "Let me get this straight. You're a groom, repairman, nurse, and gunslinger?"

"Yup. And I'm good at singing too, if people want some entertainment along the way."

"We don't," Mrs. Tucker interjected. She sat next to the window and peered out, scowling at the girl. "We want peace and quiet."

"I can give you that too," the girl said cheerfully, not seeming daunted in the least by the older woman's condescending manner toward her.

Jude struggled not to smile at her response. "There's been little evidence of that, darlin'. Now

I'm sorry, but there's no room in this coach for you. You'll have to go west on the date you scratched out on the ticket."

"There is too room!" she exclaimed. "I don't see a shotgun rider. Like I said, I can be the guard and sit with you up front. I'll keep my eye out for Pawnee and road agents, and I'll be real helpful to you. After all, I was taught how to shoot by Jesse James, the outlaw. He's one of the best guns around."

She placed a foot on the wheel, grasped the seat's metal bar, and swung up to the box. Once settled, she placed her hands in her lap, folded them, and sat with her shoulders back and her head high. She stared straight ahead as though the conversation were over and her riding along was a sure thing.

Stunned by her initiative, it took a moment for Jude to respond. He was about to swing her right back down and give her a scolding as well as a parting smack to her impertinent hind end when the senator bellowed his displeasure. "Driver, get that barrel boarder off our ride so we can be on our way! We're wasting time." He stepped inside the coach and sat down heavily next to his wife.

The girl focused pleading eyes down at Jude. He stared up at her, wondering what her real story was and why she was so determined to come along. A wounded look crossed her face after the senator's insult, but she quickly masked it and replaced it with a hopeful and slightly stubborn expression.

Jude had already decided he didn't care too much for the senator, and now he cared for him even less. There was no need for him to call the girl names, and he certainly shouldn't have bossed around a driver. Jude removed his hat and smacked it against his knee to shake off the dust, then readjusted the red bandana around his neck. As he placed his Stetson back on his head, an idea came to him. It just so happened that the girl was valuable in imparting an important lesson about who was in charge for the next twenty-six days. He addressed the senator sternly. "That's the last time you'll be giving orders if you want to stay on my coach. Also, I won't tolerate any disrespect toward the other passengers, including my new guard here. We all need to get along for the next twenty-two-hundred miles of rough travel, and squabbling will only make the journey more uncomfortable." He looked up at the girl and addressed her just as sternly. "What's your name, young lady?"

Her face lit up and split into a grin. "Miss Caroline Broderick, at your service. You can call me Callie, though, seeing as how we're gonna be working together."

Jude stifled another smile. He found her pluck rather cute, but he knew the challenges that faced them meant he couldn't be indulgent and tolerate any more misbehavior. The girl seemed half-feral, and the last thing he needed was someone causing trouble on what already might be a troublesome journey. "All right, Callie. You can be my shotgun, but that means you'll have to mind me. No more taking liberties without permission. Is that clear?"

"Yes, sir," she said eagerly. "I'll be no trouble to you whatsoever. You'll hardly know I'm here."

Jude had a strong suspicion this wouldn't be the case, but he kept that thought to himself. He also kept to himself the thought that she desperately needed a new dress to accommodate her womanly figure. The dress, obviously made to fit a girl, not a woman, was too short and too tight. Her breasts pressed against the fabric of her button-down bodice, revealing gaps between buttons. She would have been showing off most of her generous cleavage if it weren't for the chemise she wore underneath.

He turned his attention to the four passengers sitting in the coach. "On our journey, we'll encounter everything from bad weather to treacherous terrain. Worse, we might have to modify our route if word comes through to a home station alerting us to Indians or bandits. I'm not trying to scare you, but those are the facts. I need you all to agree to follow my lead. You do that, and we should all arrive to California in one piece."

"We understand," Billy said. He removed his tattered slouch hat. "My wife and I have heard good things about you, driver, and we've no problem following your lead."

"Yes, same here," Callie confirmed. "Mr. Fargo recommended you to me personally. That's why I chose to come on your coach."

Jude couldn't help but laugh then, despite the obvious lie. "Remind me to thank the boss for providing me with the pleasure of your company," he said, and winked at her.

She grinned back at him, her green eyes sparkling with delight.

CHAPTER TWO

Jude thanked the groom for tending to the horses and stepped up to the driver's seat. "Giddy-up!" he said, and the horses meandered forward, picking up speed as Jude clucked to them when they reached the wide path.

"I'll take your Colt, Mr. Johnson," the girl said. "I can't be a very good guard if I'm not heeled."

Jude gave her a sidelong glance. "Please feel free to call me Jude, and I'll keep the gun shucked for now, thank you, Callie."

She shrugged. "Suit yourself. I'm a real good aim though. Jesse James said I was better than anyone he'd ever taught before."

Jude sighed. "Our acquaintance will be much more pleasant without the tall tales."

"I'm telling the truth!" she exclaimed.

Jude shook his head. He removed his whip from his hip and held it loosely in his right hand. A short time later, he cracked it in the air that flanked the horses' right side. They sidestepped to the left smoothly, avoiding a felled tree without slowing.

"That was real impressive," Callie told him. "I'm good at aiming a whip too. My pa owned more horses than anyone else in Missouri, so I know most everything there is to know about buggies and riding. It's in my blood."

"Did your pa ever turn you over his knee for your bragging and fibbing in between raising all them horses?" he asked wryly.

"No. I never met him. And my ma died when I was seven years old. I grew up in an orphans' home. But I know all about my parents, and I turned out just like them. They were real fine folks."

That news gave him pause. "I'm sure they were," Jude said in a gentler voice. "When did you leave the orphans' home?"

"Just a couple days ago."

Jude wanted to ask what her business was in California, but he figured she would probably tell him without him needing to ask. The girl was jawing at him like she hadn't spoken to anyone in ages. Sure enough, she explained the reason for her journey next.

"I'm going to California to meet my future husband. We've been writing letters to each other for nine months now." Her voice sounded hoarse by this point in their conversation, and she coughed a few times.

Jude handed her his canteen. He'd noticed that she didn't bring along water, or any other supplies for that matter, except for a small pouch tied to her side. "Ah, so you're a catalog bride, are ya?" Jude wasn't surprised. Although passengers usually traveled in pairs, occasionally an unescorted woman would travel his line. In that case, however, she nearly always traveled with the goal of reaching a man, be it her husband or fiancé. As a result, Jude met very few women who weren't spoken for.

She nodded and took a long drink of water. "My fiancé is a miner, and he got rich off all the gold he found in California. He owns a big house with a wraparound porch and a well right out back so I won't have to lug water too far."

"Sounds fancy." He wanted to ask her more, like whether she had any proof that the man owned property, but it wasn't Jude's business. He was only responsible for getting people to their destination safely, not for ensuring their security once they arrived.

His thoughts were interrupted by a moaning sound coming from the coach. He looked behind him and saw Mrs. Tucker sticking her head out the window and panting.

"Blazes," he muttered. Sometimes he got lucky, but more often than not he had at least one passenger who felt dizzy and nauseated during the journey.

"Is she all right?" Callie asked.

Jude turned his head forward again. "Looks like she's already got traveling sickness. There's not much to be done about that, I'm afraid."

Callie fell into silence, and the only noises that could be heard then were the clip-clopping of the horses' hooves, the rubbing of metal and leather in the coach, and Mrs. Tucker retching out the window every so often.

Jude's team traveled at a gallop along the road. When the path became narrower or when the team would need to lug the coach uphill, they would have to be driven at a walk, but Jude took advantage of the clear path while he could in order to move their journey along. They needed to travel an average of eighty miles per day in order to reach their destination on time.

"Stop!" Callie called out suddenly.

Jude frowned at her. "There's no stopping for another twenty miles," he said with a raised voice over the noise of the horses' hooves.

"You *must* stop!" she shouted back at him.

He shook his head and continued to drive the horses forward. Then, to Jude's immense surprise and complete horror, the girl reached over and tugged sharply on the left rein, shouting, "Whoa!" to the horses as she did.

The horses were so confused by the contradiction between the voice command to stop and the tug on the rein to move left that the halt was haphazard at best. The two front horses understood that someone had told them to stop and so slowed their steps, but the two back horses continued on at a quick clip to the left. This caused jolting and confused whinnying until Jude was able to communicate the stop to the back horses. When the dust settled, Jude breathed a sigh of relief even as his temper flared. Disaster had been averted, but the girl's stunt could have caused injury to the horses and passengers if the coach had tipped. He lifted the brake and turned to upbraid the girl who had put everyone's safety at risk, but she'd already clambered off the coach and was running down the path in the direction from which they'd come.

"Damn and blast!" Jude stepped down. "We'll be continuing on shortly," he said through gritted teeth to the four surprised passengers as he strode past them.

"What happened? Why did the girl call for a stop?" the senator asked.

Jude continued on his way without responding because he didn't know the answer to that question. He intended to find out why in a jiffy, however. The girl was crouched on the ground. As he neared, he saw that she was pulling up a weed at the base of the stem. She tugged it free from the dirt just as Jude reached her. He placed his hands on his hips as she stood and turned to face him, beaming from ear to ear.

Jude must have looked as angry as he felt, for her triumphant expression faded when she met his gaze. Severely, he said, "You endangered my horses and the other passengers. What were you thinking, trying to take over driving?"

She blinked a few times and held out the plant timidly with an outstretched arm. "I saw this on the side of the road." Her voice was small and had a pleading quality about it.

"So?" he growled.

"It's gingerroot," she said quickly. "It will help Mrs. Tucker with her nausea."

Jude took a step toward her and held a finger to her face. "I don't care if you saw a pot of gold on the side of the road. You never, *ever* interfere with a driver's team."

"I-I'm sorry, Jude," she said, her eyes wide. "I won't do it again."

"That's for darn sure. The next home station is in Paselo. When we get there, you will no longer be welcome on the coach. Now you march your bottom back to your seat, and you keep it planted there for the rest of your short journey."

"No, please!" she cried. Her eyes filled with tears. "Please don't leave me behind in Paselo. I promise I won't be any more trouble."

Jude hated to see her cry, but he steeled himself. He couldn't tolerate such behavior from a passenger, when it could endanger the others. He had only ever kicked off two other people from his coach, and both were men who drank liquor during the journey, which was against the rules, and cursed in front of the lady passengers, also against the rules. What Callie had done was far worse, and he couldn't let it slide.

He jerked his head in the direction of the

coach, indicating that she was to move along.

Her lower lip quivered. "Please, can you punish me some other way? I have to get to California. It's the only thing I want in the whole world."

Jude's anger began to wane as he listened to her pleading. He shook his head at her, more in disbelief over what she'd done than in answer to her question.

"You can split my portion of food with the other passengers. I'll go without," she suggested.

"That's not going to happen. I don't believe in starving my passengers."

She sniffled. "Please don't leave me behind." She wiped a tear with the back of her hand, and Jude felt the last of his anger slip away. After all, her reckless action had been to help a passenger and was done in good faith. What further softened him was the fact that she did it for someone who had been less than kind to her.

"Callie," he said more gently than before, but still with a firmness in his tone. "I know you were only trying to help, and I know it's important for you to get to California. However, I can't allow behavior like that to go unpunished. What you did was out-and-out dangerous."

She nodded, a glimmer of hope creeping into her wet eyes. "I understand, Jude. But can't you give me work to do or force me to ride up top or something?"

Jude ran his hand along the beard on his

jaw and studied her. She looked like a scared and desperate child, very different from the proud little lady who had been bragging to him for the last few hours. He knew he wouldn't have the heart to leave her behind. She looked too vulnerable to be on her own, and the only punishment he thought fitting was a spanking. Yes, that's what she needed—a good blistering that would leave her temporarily sore but would impart a lasting lesson.

He folded his arms in front of his chest. "I'll tell you what, if you submit to some old-fashioned discipline, I will consider the slate wiped clean."

She blinked and stared into his eyes. "Old-fashioned discipline? Like a whipping?"

He nodded once. "Yes, like a whipping."

She looked down and took only a brief moment to decide. "All right," she said softly in the direction of the ground.

"Very well." Jude glanced at the coach behind him and noticed that the passengers had alighted and were wandering about. He was behind schedule because of the girl's stunt, and a spanking would only add more time to the delay. Still, he reckoned it was better to punish her now, ensuring a well-behaved passenger for the remainder of their journey, as opposed to waiting until they reached their first stop.

"Come with me," he said, and led the way around a bend out of sight of the other passengers. There was no need to add the humiliation of witnesses to her punishment. He stopped, unclasped his gun belt, and placed it on a rock by the side of the road.

"How far away should I walk?" she asked, her voice trembling. She looked at him fearfully.

Jude felt confused by her question. "You don't need to walk anywhere. Just turn around and bend over a little. Place your hands on your knees."

She set the weed down and obeyed. Jude couldn't help but notice how comely she looked bent over waiting for her punishment. She had shapely hips and a round, pert bottom.

She looked back at him over her shoulder. "Won't it shred my dress?"

Jude frowned, puzzled again, until it dawned on him what she was thinking. "Lands sakes! I'm not going to use my blasted horsewhip on you."

Her forehead was wrinkled into worried lines, and he felt a wave of compassion. The fact that she was willing to endure such a thing told him how strong her desire to get to California was.

"I'm going to use this belt I'm wearing." He patted the leather around the waist of his trousers. "Three licks for the stunt you pulled, that's all. It'll hurt, but nothing like a horsewhip."

When she looked at the belt, relief flooded her features. She let out a breath and turned her head forward while Jude unbuckled the belt from his hips. He folded it in half like he remembered his father doing the few times he was whipped as a boy. Jude had never given a naughty girl a licking, but it wasn't too hard to figure out how to administer it effectively. He placed a steadying hand on the small of her back and took a moment to study his lovely target, which was quite spankable in that it was plump despite her small stature. There was no doubt in his mind that the impetuous little lady deserved a licking. However, the sight of her bent over in submission to punishment brought to mind a wholly inappropriate desire to lift her dress and give her an entirely different kind of seeing-to.

"Hold still," he admonished when she fidgeted nervously in anticipation of the first stroke. "You're not to move from this position until your punishment is over, understand?"

She settled immediately. A meek "yes, sir" reached his ears.

He took a deep breath. He didn't want to spank her too hard, just enough for her to know he was serious and to make her think before behaving foolishly in the future. He drew back his arm and snapped the belt across the seat of her dress with moderate force. She let out a small yelp but remained in place.

"Good." Although he spoke the word to praise her for taking the lick without moving, he also praised himself for inflicting enough pain to cause a reaction but not enough to tempt her to break position.

Jude had a good aim and could strike a

small target from ten feet away with the end of his horsewhip every time. He practiced whipping often because it was important that a horsewhip be used with complete precision during every part of the journey. Aiming a folded belt at a girl's upended backside from less than a yard away was decidedly less complicated. That was why each lick he gave her landed in a neat line from the fleshiest part of her bottom down to the tops of her thighs, not once lashing the same spot twice.

After the three promised licks, he removed his hand from her back. She hopped from foot to foot and reached around with both hands to grab her smarting backside.

He made a last-minute decision. "You're getting one more lick for the lies you've told," Jude informed her sternly. "Get back into position."

"But... what lies?" she asked in a whine.

He scoffed. "Where do I start? How about you being taught how to shoot by Jesse James, or being taught how to nurse by Florence Nightingale?"

"But that's the truth," she protested. "I swear it."

"All right then. What about you knowing how to handle a whip on account of your pa owning more horses than everyone else in Missouri? Or being able to fix every part of a wagon?"

She hesitated for a moment, but then said with lift of her chin, "I told the truth about those things too."

Jude let out an exasperated sigh. He'd hoped she would be forthright and clear her conscience. Out of all those lies, there was only one he could prove. He stepped a few paces away and removed his horsewhip from his hip. "Come here," he ordered, as he flicked the handle with his wrist to uncoil it.

Callie trudged to him, eyeing the whip warily. He handed it to her. "If you can hit the trunk of that tree," he said, pointing at a thin baby oak about ten feet away, "I'll believe you about your whipping skills, and I won't punish you for lying. You have three tries."

The expression on the girl's face couldn't have conveyed more doubt about the task, so Jude took a few steps away to get out of the whip's range of motion. He crossed his arms and waited. Callie made an unsuccessful attempt to swing the whip, which she barely seemed able to lift. Her second attempt was slightly better in that she was able to get the whip to crack, but it landed nowhere near the target. Her third attempt was even worse than her first.

Wordlessly, Jude walked to her. He took the whip out of her hand and recoiled it as he scowled at her. Callie studiously avoided looking him in the eyes. He didn't have to ask her to assume the position again. She turned around and bent over. Jude fastened the horsewhip back on his hip and retrieved his belt. "I don't take kindly to lying.

Remember this the next time you're tempted," he growled at her, and gave her the hardest wallop of all.

"Owww!" she cried, and straightened. Jude watched her lower lip protrude into a pout as she rubbed her bottom. He didn't know why exactly he'd felt compelled to punish her for lying. It was outside of the original reason for punishment, and he certainly wouldn't have punished her for it if he weren't already in the midst of disciplining her for something else. Her behavior wasn't his concern as long as it didn't cause other people harm.

Jude finished buckling his belt. He regarded the girl with his hands on his hips and wondered what he should do with her now. He wanted to give her a hug, since she looked very cute and forlorn with her lips formed into a pout and small hands rubbing her spanked bottom. Instead of hugging her, which didn't seem proper, he reached out and flicked her lower lip gently with his thumb, which he realized wasn't proper either when the feel of her damp lip against his thumb caused him to experience a sudden desire to kiss her. "Little girls who pout after punishment get more spankings," he said in a teasing manner. Her lips morphed into a small smile, confirming that she heard the tease in his voice.

Jude smiled along with her to let her know all was forgiven. "That's better. Come along now. We are way behind schedule." He walked in the direction of the coach as she scurried to the plant she'd uprooted, picked it up, and then followed him, jogging to keep up with his long strides.

The passengers were still walking around, taking advantage of the opportunity to stretch their legs. Mrs. Tucker still looked quite green, and her discomfort didn't do anything for her temper. She scowled at Callie and then at Jude. "Are we going to be stopping often, wasting time in the middle of nowhere?" she demanded to know.

The senator complained next. "I told you to leave that girl behind. She's nothing but trouble. I don't want to suffer at the hands of a little scamp who isn't even on the right coach."

Jude frowned. "Senator Tucker, Mrs. Tucker —Callie won't be doing something so foolish again, but you might listen to what she has to say. She was only trying to help." He looked at the girl and nodded, encouraging her to provide an explanation.

Callie held up the plant proudly, as though it was a large fish she'd just caught and not a dusty weed. "This here is gingerroot." Handing it to Mrs. Tucker, she said, "Gnawing on that root might help you with your stomach trouble."

Mrs. Tucker's expression conveyed nothing but contempt for the dirty plant that had been shoved into her hands. She rolled her eyes and addressed Jude. "Can we go now?"

It broke a piece of Jude's heart when he saw Callie's face fall and her shoulders slump forward. After all that, Jude hated that she wasn't even graced with a polite thank you. "Yes, let's get to it. We have miles of ground to cover before we arrive at the station."

As the others climbed into the coach, he bent and whispered into Callie's ear, "That Mrs. Tucker is wearing the ugliest hat this side of Copes River, don't you think?"

The girl's expression changed from crestfallen to delighted, and she giggled silently, holding a hand over her mouth and nodding at him conspiratorially.

He winked at her and offered his hand to assist her ascent up to the box seat, though he knew she was perfectly limber enough to make it up herself. He didn't imagine the girl had often been treated like a lady because she climbed up awkwardly, appearing like his assistance was more of a hindrance than a help, but she made it and settled on the seat with a barely perceptible wince. They started on their way again.

Jude felt glad when Mrs. Tucker called out to Callie an hour later and told her the ginger was working and she didn't feel as sick. The girl looked over at Jude with a happy grin. "That was worth the walloping. I'm not even sore anymore."

Jude arched a brow at her. "Maybe I didn't spank you hard enough." He cracked the horsewhip in the air, moving the horses along at a faster pace than usual during this part of the journey in order to make up for time lost.

She stared at him with wide eyes. "It was

hard enough. I won't ever pull your reins again."

He chuckled at her earnest response. "I'm glad to hear that, darlin'. No more lying either, all right?"

She sighed. "All right, Jude."

CHAPTER THREE

By the time they arrived at the swing station, which was nothing more than a one-room shack and barn with a milk cow and four fresh horses, everyone felt sore and weary. Mrs. Tucker removed her hat and tossed it carelessly to the corner, causing Jude to grin and silently congratulate himself. She'd gotten sick of the hat even sooner than he'd thought she would.

The groom who lived at the station provided the group with a bland meal of beans and potatoes, which they relished without a word of complaint. One thing Jude had discovered during his days in the army and on the line was that there's no spice that can make food more delicious than hunger. Conversation between himself and the passengers flowed easily.

"I hear there are two seasons in California —summer and preparing for summer. Sounds like heaven," Annie said with a wistful sigh.

"Well, I don't know about that," Mrs. Tucker countered. "I don't care much for winter, but the heat causes me to feel faint."

The senator cleared his throat. "It's a dry heat in California, dear. Much different from the humid climate we're used to. What feels like a hundred degrees in Missouri feels like a balmy seventy in California."

"That sounds mighty fine," Billy piped up. "If I wasn't already sold on California, I would be after hearing that. The weather is something nice to look forward to after the discomfort of travel. I swear, I'd rather get caught in a tornado than ever travel by coach again. No offense, Jude."

"None taken."

"The driver's seat is the most comfortable. That and the girl's," the senator commented, saying *the girl* with undisguised derision and resentment.

Callie spoke for the first time then. "I'd think you'd be comfortable wherever you sat, Senator Tucker, seeing as how you have plenty of built-in cushioning on your person."

Jude choked on the drink of water he was swallowing, the female passengers gasped, and a red anger flushed the senator's cheeks. Like when she'd brazenly climbed up to the box seat, Jude once again found himself in a state of stunned silence over the girl's behavior which, while shocking, was becoming more and more predictable in its inappropriateness. He didn't want to scold her in front of the other passengers, but he made a mental note to discuss manners with her in the near future.

Quelling the tension, Annie changed the subject to mending, letting the passengers know she had a small sewing kit in her parcel should anyone need some patching during the journey. Callie didn't speak again, and Jude noticed her slipping out of the shack after eating her meal.

It was decided that the men and Callie would sleep on the hardwood floor, each with one blanket and a small straw-stuffed pillow. There were only two cots, which were offered to Mrs. Tucker and Annie. Callie wasn't considered for a cot because she'd been riding in the most comfortable seat on the stagecoach. The senator continued to grumble about the disparity of her prime seating arrangement in comparison to theirs, and Jude reckoned he should switch her out with the others occasionally in order to keep peace on the journey.

When Callie didn't return after some time, Jude grew worried. He glanced around the room and noticed that everyone seemed to be asleep, but he wasn't able to relax not knowing where she was. He exited quietly and headed for the barn, which was only a few paces north of the shack. He saw the glow of a lamp through the cracks of the door. When he pulled the door open, he spotted Callie on the ground next to one of the horses with her knees pulled to her chest. Her back was turned to him, and she rocked back and forth humming to herself. The coal oil lamp burned nearby, casting a glow on her head. Something about Callie's pose, which seemed small and afraid, made his concern grow.

"Callie," he called to her softly. "You all right?"

Looking back, she nodded at him but didn't speak.

Jude approached her cautiously, as though she was a rabbit who might bolt at any moment. He crouched and placed a hand on her back. "Come to the cabin now. It's time to get some shut-eye."

Callie shook her head. "Nah, Jude. You don't want me there, trust me. I'll sleep out here."

Jude could see that she needed some convincing to return with him, though he didn't have any idea why. He sat on the hay-covered ground next to her. "What are you talking about? You should be sleeping in the cabin with the other passengers, not out here alone in the barn."

"I'm not alone," she said, looking pointedly at the horse next to her.

"You know what I mean. Why don't you want to come inside? I won't let anyone treat you poorly, if that's what you're worried about."

She looked over and gave him a small smile. "Thank you, Jude. It's not that. The thing is, I have a strange malady that will keep others from being able to sleep."

"Oh? And what is it?"

She hesitated, obviously not wanting to share, but she took a deep breath and said, "I don't like the dark. I panic. I can't handle the quiet so I have to make noise."

Jude didn't understand. "Noise?"

"I have to hum or tap my foot or do something whenever it's dark and quiet, like when others are sleeping. Sometimes it's not enough and I end up screaming. Believe me, I've tried not to. It annoys people something fierce, but I just can't help myself. I'd wake people up and they'd be sore at me."

It was the strangest affliction Jude had ever heard of, but the way she communicated it reluctantly to him with some embarrassment in her voice told him that she was serious and that it really was something she couldn't help.

"I know I'm addled," she lamented. "I worry that Albert won't like me when he finds out about this."

"Balderdash," Jude said, his voice firm. "It's a little odd, I will admit, but everyone has their peculiarities."

"Some peculiarities are more peculiar than others, though." She looked down and fiddled with the hem of her worn dress.

Jude rose to his feet and held out his hand to her. "Come along. I won't have you spending the night out here alone."

"But Jude—"

"No point arguing, Callie, my mind is made up. Take my hand now." He spoke to her as he would a child whose only choice was obedience.

Callie sighed and slowly reached up. Jude enclosed her small hand in his much larger one and tugged her to her feet. He led her out of the barn and headed for the shack. She dragged her feet a pace behind him, obviously reluctant to go with him.

He stopped walking. "Look, young lady," he said in a disapproving voice. "You'd better stop acting like a stubborn child or I'll take you back to the barn and give you your second spanking of the day. Is that what you want?"

She let out a whimper and looked down. "No."

"Then stop dragging your feet." He resumed the walk, and she fell into step beside him. He gave her hand a squeeze. "I don't mean to sound unkind, and you'll have to forgive my bossiness. You seem so young and alone in this big world. I feel I must look after you until it becomes your husband's job."

She didn't immediately respond. As they reached the door, he felt her squeeze his hand in return. "I'm glad I met you, Jude, even if you are a bit bossy."

❉ ❉ ❉

Callie lay on her back atop her assigned blanket, staring at the darkness above her. Jude had shown her to her spot on the floor, which was a body's length away from where he slept. She remained quiet for several minutes, but as she lay there in the noiseless dark, her panic formed and grew steadily. It started in the pit of her stomach and rose to her chest. Her heartbeat picked up speed and she felt frantic. It was too quiet. She had to hear something! With tears streaming down her cheeks, she began to hum as quietly as she could, but the hum built in volume along with her terror.

Before long, the senator was awake and not at all happy about it. "Shut up, you useless waste of space!"

Annie was politer in her admonishment, but her annoyance was just as apparent. "Hush now, girl. We're trying to sleep."

Callie was able to stop humming momentarily, but a short time later the panic compelled her to resume. Angry grumbling could be heard from the passengers, and Callie wondered if Jude would notice if she snuck out and slept in the barn as she originally intended.

As though summoned by her thoughts, she felt the warmth of Jude's body by her side. He touched her cheek lightly with the back of his hand, which caused her to flinch.

"Easy. It's going to be all right," he said softly. He wiped a tear off her cheek with the pad of his thumb. "I have an idea." He laced his fingers through her hair and cupped her head. Then he brushed his thumb back and forth over her ear's opening, creating a sound like a loud rushing river. After less than a minute, her heartbeat slowed and her panting eased into normal breathing.

"That's it," he said. "I'm going to keep doing this until you fall asleep, darlin'. Close your eyes."

Callie felt incredibly touched by the gesture and impressed by the ingenuity of it. "Thank you," she whispered to him. Now that the panic was gone, she realized just how tired she was. It had been a very long day, and she drifted into sleep with the comforting sounds of a river next to her ear.

CHAPTER FOUR

Callie startled awake. She rubbed her eyes and glanced around the room. The passengers milled about, rolling up their blankets and engaging in small talk with each other. Jude stood nearby rolling up his blanket also. His back faced her, and she studied the outline of his broad shoulders against the streaming light of the window in front of him. He'd already donned his gun belt and whip and looked ready to light out in a hurry.

The way he looked—so strong and capable—made a feeling grow inside Callie that she'd never known before. Her skin prickled and her body came to life even as she retreated farther under her blanket, fearful of her sudden attraction toward him. She recalled the strength in his voice when he directed the horses and the way he cracked the whip with such authority, and she felt a magnetic draw to his power. The feeling was so intense that she had to convince herself to remain still as opposed to launching herself into his arms. She wasn't exactly versed in proper behavior around a man, but she knew initiating a hug would be frowned on. She wanted Jude to like her, not be appalled by her behavior any more than he was already.

She tried to make sense of the feelings brewing inside of her. Jude had shown her kindness just as Sam had done, but Callie looked at Jude differently than she looked at Sam. She knew this was partly because Jude was closer to her age and very handsome. She liked the sweep of dark hair over his brow when he removed his hat and the strong outline of his jaw under his neatly trimmed beard. His honey brown eyes caused her stomach to flop when directed at her, whether in a hard stare or twinkle.

Callie wondered how long she could get away with lying on her blanket daydreaming. She didn't want to speak with anyone except for Jude, knowing people would likely be annoyed with her after she woke them with her humming. She thought about apologizing, but that wasn't something she felt comfortable doing. Apologizing would make her vulnerable and at people's mercy in that they could choose not to forgive her. It had always worked better in her favor to act blameless. People's mercy was not something she'd ever been able to count on.

Suddenly the senator's form blocked Jude's. Callie moved her gaze from his hard, steel-toed boots up to his equally hard face. He regarded her without a trace of kindness, or even civility. "You'll give up your seat in the box today," he said to her in a harsh whisper. "The driver seems to have taken a shine to you for some unknown reason, but you aren't even supposed to be on this ride."

"I'm the guard," Callie said with a frown. "I have to sit in the front to be Jude's lookout."

The senator crouched down and got in her face. "You'd better think smart and take your place in the coach. If you don't, I promise you'll be sorry." His voice was threatening, and Callie would have felt afraid if Jude wasn't only a few steps away.

She considered giving up her seat for only a brief moment. She wanted more than just about anything to sit up front with Jude again. "I'm sitting in the box," she snarled, scrambling to her feet and facing him with a proud lift of her chin. She raised her voice. "You're a bully and an ass, and I won't be cowed by you," she told him in a louder voice than she'd intended. Annie gasped at her language, and Jude focused a disapproving look in her direction.

Callie turned her back to them all and proceeded to roll her blanket. She could feel the senator's gaze on her, heating her back with his hatred, and it sent a shiver of fear down her spine. She knew he was a cruel man. She'd seen that look before—the stony look in a person's eyes that held not an iota of compassion. It was the same look she saw in Mrs. Bentley's eyes, and she was familiar with the dangers associated with getting on such a person's bad side. Still, she felt she had an ally in

Jude, so that gave her enough courage to stand her ground.

"All right, everyone, listen up," Jude's authoritative voice rang out, interrupting the silent battle she was waging with the senator.

Callie turned to face Jude, as did everyone else. She was in the back of the room, and the senator stood in front of her, with his watch hanging slightly over his pocket. She had the sudden desire to swipe it. There was no reason for this desire except for her dislike of the man, but the urge to steal it felt uncontrollable. Glancing around quickly to make sure no one was watching, she reached out and took it discreetly. She shoved it in her suede pouch and felt a thrill of triumph.

Jude stood with his hands on his hips, a pose that was becoming familiar to Callie. It made him look casual and commanding at the same time. "We've got eighty miles between here and the Copes River. There we will stock up on water and rest the horses for only three hours before continuing on. Then it's another hundred miles of rough travel before we stop to sleep in a hotel in Paselo. That means we'll be traveling overnight, so you'll need to sleep in the coach, if at all. Any questions?"

The senator responded in a cordial manner, quite differently from how he had just addressed Callie. "Driver, I think I speak for all of us when I say we are grateful for your leadership, which I have no cause to believe is anything but fair and equitable. On that point, I do believe it reasonable that one of us be offered a seat in the box for this next part of the journey. The girl has had more than enough time in the prime seat."

"I'm supposed to sit in the box," Callie argued, anger lacing her words. "I'm the guard."

The senator didn't even look at her. Instead his attention remained on Jude. The expression on Jude's face stayed the same, but his voice sounded annoyed when he spoke. "Very well, Senator. Callie will sit in the coach for the next eighty miles, and one of you may join me in the front. Decide the person among yourselves. It makes no difference to me. Let's get a move on now, folks. Breakfast will be served outside by the coach. No dilly-dallying."

Callie's heart sank, and she felt stung by Jude's decision. It hurt her feelings that he didn't put up any resistance to someone else sitting by him. The smug look that the senator shot at her added anger to her hurt feelings. She gritted her teeth and strode outside, pointedly avoiding looking at Jude as she stormed past him, but she saw out of the corner of her eye that he was observing her with his hands on his hips.

Outside, the groom buckled the straps to the horses' harness, while the passengers ate their portions of bread and milk. They stood around the coach and chatted with each other, but Callie had no interest in participating. She collected her breakfast and walked away from them. She wanted to be alone.

Jude noticed her retreat and called to her, "We're leaving in less than five minutes, Callie. Don't be going anywhere."

She ignored him and strode to the barn, where she meandered around to the back out of sight and continued to a thicket of trees. After she'd bolted down her fare, she reached inside her pouch and pulled out one of the letters from Albert. The border of the paper was worn and smudged with her fingerprints from handling it so often. She had memorized each line, but she still liked to read her favorite parts often.

Thank you for sending your photograph, Callie. As I suspected, you are quite a lovely miss. I'm sorry for not having a likeness of myself to share with you at this time, but I shall describe my looks to the best of my ability. I am of slightly above-average height with even features, light skin, and blond hair. I am not sure how else to describe myself, but I hope you won't be disappointed. I don't believe I'm a bad-looking man, though from looking at your picture, I can see that you are far lovelier than I am handsome.

Callie smiled, sighed, and held the letter to her chest. His words gave her comfort. She didn't honestly care much about what Albert looked like, only that he would find her comely and be kind to her. She reckoned that particular paragraph from his letter told her all she needed to know about him, and it filled her with great hope for her future.

Callie lost track of the time she spent apart from the others. She suddenly became aware of a bugle sounding and voices calling for her. The voices didn't sound all too pleased. In fact, they sounded downright angry. This was confirmed when she heard the crackling of a weed beneath a heavy footstep and turned around to find Jude approaching her looking as tetchy as a teased snake. Her heart skipped a beat, and she rushed to apologize. "I'm sorry, Jude. I just realized people were calling for me. My mind was elsewhere."

"I told you not to go anywhere, and you pointedly ignored me. I would have let it slide if you'd come back in a decent amount of time." He took hold of her arm and dragged her out of the thicket into the barn. She tried to pull away, but his grip was firm. He sat on a bench and hauled her over his lap.

She wailed another apology. "I'm sorry. Please don't spank me, Jude!"

He tossed up her skirt and petticoat as she squirmed. "You decided to run off like a child when you didn't get your way, so you'll be treated as one," he growled. He landed a hard swat over her thin drawers, nearly covering the entirety of her bottom with his large hand. "Other people want to sit up front, and you're going to have a good attitude about it by the time I get through with you. You're also going to mind my words when I speak." He punctuated his admonishment with hard swats that jerked her forward each time.

"I'll mind you! And I'll have a good attitude." She squirmed frantically over his lap as his hand picked up speed and fell again and again.

"Hold still," he said sternly, landing two sharp swats on her thighs, "or I'll remove your drawers and blister you with my belt."

She gasped, mortified, and stopped jerking about momentarily, but his swats were so hard that she found it nearly impossible to remain still. This punishment felt much worse than when he'd landed the belt four times over the protection of her skirts, and it sure lasted a lot longer than the first spanking. Jude grasped her waist and pulled her against his body to keep her from twisting off his lap. The smacks were loud and echoed against the walls of the barn. The horses and cow neighed and mooed along with her howls.

Jude brought his hand down with great focus, not letting up for quite some time and making sure every inch of her bottom received punishment. He lectured her as he spanked, but Callie barely heard it, being so focused on the sting, which deepened with each fall of his hand. "You will stay with the others. I'll not have you running off, worrying me and delaying our trip." *Smack!*

"I'll stay with the others!" she promised in a wail.

"That you will, young lady." He smacked the low curve of her bottom especially hard. "Otherwise, you'll be spending the entire trip sitting on a smarting bottom. Is that what you want?"

"No," she hiccupped, hating that tears were coursing down her face. She watched one drip on the ground next to Jude's dusty boot. In addition to feeling pained, she also felt terribly angry and betrayed. She thought Jude was her friend, but instead of being friendly, he was giving her a very painful spanking, and after this, he was going to allow another passenger to take her place up front. She thought he liked her and wanted to sit with her, but he mustn't think much of her at all if he felt inclined to cause her such agony.

Jude stopped spanking. He ran his hand over her scorched backside and rested it on her thigh. "One more thing. The senator is bellowing that you stole his pocket watch. I really don't want to believe him."

His touch felt gentle now, and she might have relaxed had it not been for his statement. Her heart sank, and she deeply regretted her impulsive theft. She searched for the words to say but couldn't find them. Jude hadn't exactly asked her if she'd taken the watch, and she certainly wasn't going to offer him a confession, which as good as guaranteed more time in her current position. Callie remained silent, figuring that was the safest option.

Jude sighed heavily, then righted her skirts and planted her on her feet in front of him. He held her arms and studied her, frowning. "Think you can behave now?"

Callie shrugged out of his grasp and swiped at her tears with the backs of her hands. "I hate you." The words were spoken hesitantly in a trembling voice. She worried the pronouncement might get her spanked again, but it was the only thing she wanted to say to him.

Jude's eyebrows lifted. "You can hate me, darlin'. What you can't do is disobey me."

"Fine. You've made your point," she spat and turned away. She felt humiliated, and her face felt nearly as hot as her bottom. She needed to get away from the man who had so unfairly chastised her. How could she have been foolish enough to believe he liked her? Hardly anyone liked her. She rushed out of the barn toward the coach. Much to her dismay, Jude's long strides caught up with her, and he walked by her side. She wiped away the rest of her tears, hoping no one would guess she'd just been spanked. Everyone regarded her angrily as she approached. Feeling embarrassed, lonely, and misunderstood, she climbed into the coach, gingerly scooted to the far end, and retrieved a letter from Albert, which she proceeded to focus on while everyone else stepped in.

The senator took the box seat; his snooty wife sat next to Callie. A short time later, the coach lurched forward. Callie read her letters from

Albert over and over before finally putting them back in the pouch. When she looked across the seat at Billy and Annie who faced her, she found them regarding her warily, like one might a stray dog. Callie decided she didn't wish to speak to them. They didn't seem interested in speaking with her either and instead talked between themselves and with Mrs. Tucker. Callie closed her eyes and pretended to sleep while daydreaming about her future with Albert and lamenting her poor spanked bottom.

CHAPTER FIVE

The coach finally came to a halt after what seemed like ages. The passengers groaned as they exited. Everyone felt stiff and sore after this part of the journey, which was quite bumpy, and they stretched and bemoaned the aches in their body. Callie walked a ways off to do the necessary, her bladder feeling like it might burst at any moment. She made sure to rejoin the others immediately after she relieved herself, not wanted to draw Jude's ire again for removing herself from the party. He didn't seem to notice her, though. She didn't see him so much as glance in her direction as he unhooked the horses and rubbed them down.

Mrs. Tucker and Annie rolled out a blanket on the ground and laid upon it, intending to sleep for the three hours they would be camped there, while the male passengers walked alongside the river to stretch their legs. Callie didn't wish to nap with the other women, nor did she wish to exercise with the male passengers, so she felt at a loss over what to do. She didn't feel like she belonged with anyone, and she felt a wave of loneliness. She often felt this way, like an outcast who would never fit in no matter where she went. To her mind, this would all change when she arrived in California and became Albert's wife. Then she would have a purpose, and she would finally belong to someone.

Briefly, she wondered if Jude would permit her to hike along the river on her own as long as she made it back in time to resume the journey, but she didn't want to ask his permission. She didn't want to talk to him ever again in fact. Frustrated, Callie took to pacing around the camp within sight of the coach. When she grew tired of that, she walked to the riverfront and sat on a large rock, which was still within sight of Jude and the horses. She skipped small stones across the water but couldn't get them to skip more than twice. Still she continued idly tossing the rocks, grateful for the activity. She became so entranced by the sunset over the river that caused the water to sparkle that she didn't hear the footsteps that approached her from behind.

"If you use a flat stone and snap your wrist sideways, you'll have more luck getting them to skip."

Callie looked over her shoulder at Jude and followed him with her gaze as he walked around and sat down next to her on the rock. He opened his fist, revealing a collection of flat stones, and gave her an encouraging nod. She picked up one of the rocks from his palm. Drawing her hand back, she snapped her wrist and let it fly. It skipped four times. She couldn't help but smile a little after the minor accomplishment. He returned the smile and poured the rest of the flat stones he'd collected into her hands. She felt a trickle of warmth toward him. It was a small gift, but she didn't often receive gifts at all.

"You're sulking, darlin'," he remarked.

She sat up a little straighter. "I'm not. I'm just sitting here minding my own business."

"Minding your own business and sulking," he insisted.

"Think what you like," she said stiffly.

"I know you're still mad at me for spanking you, and I don't like to see you angry." He rubbed the back of his neck, appearing conflicted.

She felt angry, yes, but more so her feelings were hurt. She glared at him. "My fiancé would never treat me brutishly as you have. I can't wait 'til I'm in California where I'll be treated like a lady."

Jude stood and skipped a rock across the river four times, then turned to face her. "I sure hope your fiancé treats you well. You deserve a fair shake."

"He will treat me just fine," she said firmly. "Albert is a gentleman."

"I'm glad, honey."

Callie's temper flared. "Don't be nice to me, Jude! Don't call me darling and honey! You can't be nice one minute, making me think you like me, and then hit me the next. It's got me all confused and I don't like it."

He frowned at her and cocked his head. "I don't quite see it that way. I wouldn't spank someone I didn't like. I like you quite a lot."

"Why would you hurt me if you like me? That makes no sense."

"Of course it does. I want you safe and well behaved so you can have the best life possible, and sometimes a little temporary pain prevents a world of hurt in the future. Hasn't anyone ever looked out for you and corrected your behavior?"

Callie felt a lump rising in her chest, which she gulped down. She wouldn't allow herself to cry again in front of Jude, although that's exactly what she felt like doing after hearing his question. She hadn't had much in the way of someone looking out for her since her mother died—only one person in fact. She lifted her chin a little higher. "There was someone... Sam. He watched out for me, but he never spanked me like you've done."

"I'm glad someone looked after you. Tell me about this Sam fellow."

Callie didn't know why Jude cared to hear about him, but she didn't mind talking about her friend. She missed him, and thinking of him brought a sort of melancholy that felt nice to dwell upon. "He's a cowhand I met shortly after my mother passed. Anytime I needed a meal after being locked in the closet for a long time without food or water, he'd go and buy it for me. He wanted to take me home and raise me with his kids, but his wife said they couldn't afford another mouth to feed."

A surprised look crossed Jude's face, followed by a look of sadness. "You were locked in a closet?"

Callie returned her gaze to the river and shrugged. "You look just like how Sam looked when I told him about the closet—all worried. It was awful being locked in there, but what kept my spirits up was knowing that I had a friend in Sam. He was the one who pointed out the mail-order bride posting in the paper. He wanted me to have a better life."

"I see. Sounds like he was a good friend to you." Jude's voice sounded mournful.

Callie bristled. She could tell that Jude was feeling sorry for her, and she didn't like that. She wanted people to respect her, to be impressed by her, not to look down on her as having less than them. She felt exposed and angry once again.

"Sam was like the pa I never had. I hated his children. I wanted them to die so I could take their place."

It was a spiteful thing to say, and she expected Jude to scold her for that and stop feeling pity, but that wasn't what happened. He saw right through her words and sounded even more sympathetic.

"I'm sorry, honey. You deserved a pa of your very own."

Callie felt the lump rising higher, up to her throat. She swallowed it down again and scowled in the direction of the river. She willed for him to walk away and leave her alone, but instead he walked back to her and sat down again.

He didn't say anything, and they sat in silence for some time until Callie blurted, "Sam did threaten to give me a licking a couple times. He never went through with it, though. He felt bad about the way I was getting treated at the home."

Jude nodded and scrubbed a hand around his beard. "I reckon he did right by you. Seems you needed to be shown more mercy than justice at the time. As a result of very little care and discipline, however, you've turned into a bit of a hellion."

Callie's eyes snapped to Jude's face. "I don't mean to be."

"Oh, you do a little," he said with a small smile. "You must know calling the senator an ass was impolite at best, and it's not good manners to point out when someone is overweight."

"He's a horrible man," she stated, without remorse.

"That may be true," Jude said, becoming serious again, though his voice remained gentle. "But as my father used to say, when it's hardest to be a good person, that's when it's most important. Treating people rudely is wrong, even if it feels good at the time to do so."

Callie stared at her hands. No one had ever lectured her like Jude was doing, insisting that she act a certain way, with what seemed to be no motive other than to help her be a better person.

Jude wasn't finished. "It's also not proper to sulk for hours after a punishment, even if that's what you feel like doing. The point of punishment is to learn from it and modify how you behave going forward."

Callie felt tears forming, which she quickly blinked away. "What does it matter to you how I behave?"

"Believe it or not, darlin', I meant what I said about liking you a lot. I want you to have a good life and good people around you. But that starts with you. You have to be the kind of person who acts respectfully toward others in order to acquire their respect. If you act like a hellion, you're going to attract other hellions."

Callie plucked at her shoe straps, avoiding Jude's gaze, and said quietly, "I want to be a good person. I will act better when I marry Albert."

"There's no better time than now to start acting properly. What makes you think you will change after getting married?"

"I'll live a quiet life in my new home, baking bread and churning butter—you know, doing all the things wives do. I'll mend my husband's clothes and bake him pies. There won't be any need to defend myself or hitch rides on coaches. My husband will support me, and people will think I'm important because I'm Albert's wife."

Jude smiled. "You're important already, but

you're going to be a fine wife too, Callie. I can tell."

She looked up and gave him a shy smile back. "Thanks." Her hurt feelings faded away, and she decided Jude wasn't so bad after all. He was strict with her, and she wasn't used to his kind of discipline, but she was convinced once again that he liked her. This was important to her, she realized. As with Sam, she felt drawn to Jude and the kindness he'd shown her. Unlike with Sam, however, she felt more a woman than a girl around him, and when he looked at her, she desperately desired for him to be pleased with what he saw.

Jude sobered. "Now I know I've been hard on you, but I'm your friend just like Sam was. I'll watch out for you, and if that bootlickin' senator or anyone else mistreats you, let me know, ya hear? They'll have to answer to me. And I want you to promise me you'll behave and act respectfully toward the others from now on. I know you can do it."

Callie felt a wave of uncharitable happiness, knowing Jude didn't like the senator either. "All right," she agreed. "Will you promise not to spank me again? I don't like it."

Jude raised an eyebrow. "You're not supposed to like it, and I'll make no such promise. I think we've already established that part of looking out for you includes making sure you behave and doling out consequences if you don't." He stood and reached down to cup her chin, tilting her face upward so he could look into her eyes. "Be a good girl and I won't have any cause to redden that cute caboose of yours again."

Callie felt a thrill travel straight to her loins, despite also feeling annoyed that he wouldn't promise to not spank her. She liked that he called her bottom cute, and she felt aroused by the embarrassing yet titillating words. "I'll do my best," she said. "Have you looked after other passengers before?" The thought that he provided any other woman with the same attention caused a burst of unexpected jealousy to bloom in her chest, similar to how she felt when she thought about Sam's children.

He chuckled and released her chin. "Not in the same way, but then I've never met another passenger quite like you before. You're strong and grown up in some ways but fragile and unruly like a child in others. I get the hankerin' to kiss you and spank you at the same time."

Her eyes widened, taken aback that he would make such a declaration when she was engaged to another. He seemed to notice her surprise because he held up his hand. "Don't get your dander up, I won't take liberties with kissing you, only spanking. Your future husband will thank me for that, but he'd likely kill me for doing the other."

She felt strangely disappointed over his promise not to kiss her, though she knew it was only proper. She wondered how it would feel for him to press his mouth to hers. Would he be gentle and just brush her lips, or would his tongue take possession of her mouth boldly?

Ashamed of her wanton thoughts, she pushed them away. She'd no sooner done so when she felt another stab of guilt over stealing the senator's pocket watch. Jude seemed pleased with her now, and she wanted him to remain that way, but she also wanted him to know the truth and forgive her. It took some courage, but she reached inside her pouch and slowly drew out the watch.

"The senator was right about me stealing it. I'm sorry, Jude," she said quietly as she held it out to him. She searched his face as he took it from her.

Jude studied the watch in his hand for a moment with a frown, appearing deep in thought. She swallowed hard and waited for his verdict. When he spoke after a long, excruciating silence, it was in a stern voice that made her heart beat a little faster in her chest.

"I'm proud of you for confessing, Callie, especially knowing it could earn you another punishment, but this is serious. If thieving is a habit of yours, I suggest you break it now. Stealing is wrong, even if it's from a bad man, and if I catch you at it again on this journey, I'll give you a licking you won't forget. Understand?"

Callie blinked back tears. It felt awful being scolded again after she'd experienced him being pleased with her. Now he seemed disappointed once more. She nodded and looked down.

A moment later he flicked her lower lip with

his thumb. "Pouting again," he said in his teasing voice.

She felt relieved at his lighthearted tone and felt even better when she looked up at him. His eyes were warm and kind, and he smiled at her. "I'll smooth this over with the senator, darlin'. Cheer up. Like I said, I'm proud of you for confessing. I just need you not to steal again."

"Oh, I won't, Jude!" she exclaimed, and she wouldn't. He gave her a satisfied nod before returning to his team of horses. A short time later, he blew the bugle, signaling that it was time to move on.

Callie walked to the coach with a spring in her step, her hopes high that she'd be allowed to sit in the box again with Jude. He was already up in his seat, and Mrs. Tucker stood below and spoke up at him. Callie felt her temper boil and her hope evaporate. She knew the woman was asking to ride up front. She watched with dismay as Jude nodded, reached down, and helped her up by grasping her arm. In a fluid motion, he maneuvered her around his legs and helped her to settle next to him.

Callie stormed to the coach, looking once at Jude to find him staring at her. She shot him an angry look, and he returned a stern one with eyebrow raised. She felt her stomach flop. The man didn't even have to use words. She knew he'd just let her know she'd better not make a fuss, or else. Sighing, she climbed into the coach next to the senator, who wasted no time in expressing his dislike of her.

"Glad you aren't dawdling for once far away from the coach when we're ready to leave," he snarled. His face scrunched into a look of contempt. He pointedly drew his handkerchief over his nose to indicate that she was beneath him, a dirty lowlife.

"Go to blazes, you crusty old curmudgeon," she hissed. She stiffened after saying that and desperately hoped Jude hadn't heard. He'd just explained how he expected her to behave and she'd barely gone two minutes without being rude. She relaxed when the coach moved forward. Once again they were on their way to California, where all her dreams would come true.

CHAPTER SIX

At first Jude drove the horses at only a walk, but then he pushed them into a gallop along the smooth road. When the road became rough, he again slowed the horses to a walk. It was obvious that Jude was very good at driving, and Callie found herself admiring him without even seeing his work. She knew he snapped the whip at just the right time, always with the safety of the horses and passengers in mind.

After they'd traveled what seemed like a million miles, Callie felt like she was about to crawl out of her skin. She wanted nothing more than to join Jude, who would converse with her unlike the other passengers. A plan formed in her mind about how to get back in her rightful seat. It involved annoying the passengers, which would go against Jude's admonishment to treat people respectfully, but it would cause no harm. If her plan worked, Jude might scold or even spank her, but that would be bearable if it would get her back in the box.

And so Callie began humming in the way that annoyed the passengers when they'd slept over at the swing station. They hushed her, but she continued and added a tap of her foot on the floor to increase their annoyance. Annie begged her to be quiet in her gentle way. "Let's have some quiet now, Callie."

The senator was not so gentle. "Shut up, you rotten mauk, or so help me, I'll throw you out the window." He grabbed her arm and seemed quite prepared to make good on his threat until Billy spoke firmly to him.

"Let the girl go."

The senator hesitated to acquiesce but eventually flung her arm away from him. Callie rubbed it and resumed humming. Billy and Annie exchanged frustrated looks, and the senator looked mad enough to bite himself. Callie then broke into loud song. It was nearly dark by this time, and the passengers had arranged themselves as though to try to sleep, but Callie made sure her voice sounded like someone forgot to grease the wagon, which prevented them from napping.

Finally, after what seemed like hours of effort to annoy them, the senator leaned out the window. "Driver!" he shouted. "You'd better stop before a murder happens back here."

Jude didn't hear him at first, so the senator shouted again, louder. "Driver!"

Much to Callie's glee, Jude called for his horses to halt. Her heartbeat quickened with excitement. This was the only interesting activity to happen for hours.

"What is it?" Jude snapped at the senator, sounding thoroughly displeased at having the journey interrupted.

"This girl will not shut up and we're trying to sleep! We want her out of here." The senator bellowed at his wife then. "Virginia, you get down from there so the ill-mannered scamp can join the driver. Let her be his problem."

It was all Callie could do not to clap her hands with delight. Her plan was working out perfectly. The senator's wife grumbled about it, but she stepped down from her spot and swung open the coach door. The senator shoved Callie out roughly, causing her to tumble and fall on her backside. She wasn't expecting that treatment and let out an outraged shriek, though the fall didn't injure her.

"What in tarnation?" Jude exclaimed. He pulled his brake and stepped down from his seat. "Are you all right?" he asked, holding out a hand and helping Callie to her feet.

She nodded. "Yes, I suppose. The senator was real anxious to get me out of there." She pouted at Jude to appear especially victimized and brushed off the dust from her dress.

Jude frowned at her and pointed at the box to indicate that she was to get herself seated. She climbed up and smirked as she listened to Jude dressing down the senator. His voice sounded angry as he threatened to have the man removed from the party. He said that regardless of what she'd done, shoving a passenger out of a coach was unacceptable and wouldn't be tolerated. She felt vindicated that Jude had taken her side over the senator's—that is, until he climbed up next to her and informed her of her fate.

"Paselo is another four hours away. You can spend that time enjoying sitting comfortably because once we get there, I'm going to take my belt to you. Your disobedient backside will feel every bump along the road for days."

Her eyes widened, and her forlorn act became real. She didn't think what she'd done would make him that angry. "But I didn't mean—"

"I don't want to hear it. I suggest you hobble your lip, as I suspect anything you say will only get you into more trouble." He released the brake and slapped the reins over the horses.

The only light was from the moon, but it was bright enough for Callie to see how solemn Jude looked. He didn't speak with her. Every time Callie looked over at him, she regretted what she'd done a little more. She worried about the punishment, but mostly she worried that he didn't like her anymore. Finally, after being ignored for far too long, she begged, "Please forgive me. I can't bear you being angry with me."

"You will have to bear my anger, Callie," he said in a low, even voice, "and you will also have to suffer a punishment. We just discussed this! I expected you to behave, and you did the opposite."

"But I wanted to be up here with you, that's

all! I didn't cause anyone harm, and I hate sitting in the coach because no one likes me. Do you still like me?" She hated how weak the question made her sound, but she felt desperate to know.

When Jude didn't answer, tears flooded her eyes. A stab of loneliness tore at her heart. Her thoughts flashed to Sam, her best friend who she would never see again. Then she thought of her future husband. Oh, how she longed to meet him. In her mind, Albert held the answer to everything —she would never pull such a stunt with him and therefore he would always love her.

She turned her head away from Jude and sniffled quietly as her nose began to run from crying. She hoped Jude wouldn't hear her. He did, however, because he reached over, took hold of her wrist, and pulled her to him gently. He wrapped his arm around her shoulders and gave her a hug. "I like you, honey, but I don't want you to think I like your behavior. I'm disappointed in you because I know you can be good if you try. Does that make sense?"

Callie felt great relief, hearing that Jude still liked her, and she marveled over how good it felt to have his arm around her. She nodded. "Yes."

"Good. Stop carrying on then." Jude removed his arm from around her so he could hold the reins again with two hands, but Callie remained close to him. Her relief transformed to weariness. Her head dropped forward in a moment of sleep, which she startled awake from.

"Lay your head down on my leg, Callie, and try to find sleep," Jude ordered. "The next couple hours will be smooth without much rough and tumble."

She did as she was told. She placed her head on his thigh and stretched her legs across the seat. She felt his leg muscles ripple against her cheek. His thigh felt hard as a rock, but Callie didn't think she'd ever felt something more comfortable. He placed his hand lightly on her forehead and smoothed away the hair from her face. A small tremor of delight coursed through her. She couldn't recall anyone having touched her in such a way, and she felt something quite unfamiliar. She felt safe and cared for, like she always imagined children with parents felt. It didn't take long for her to fall asleep.

* * *

Callie watched Jude close the door behind them, turn up the light of the oil lamp, and peruse the room, which was sparse in its furnishings. A bed took up one corner, while another housed a small table with basin and water pitcher. The curtains over the window were brown with lace stitched around them. Jude didn't speak, and she grew nervous. It was entirely improper for an unmarried man and woman to share a private hotel room, but they had little choice. When they reached Paselo's Main Street Inn, they discovered that only three rooms were available. The couples took temporary residence in the other two rooms, leaving Callie and Jude to share the third.

But it wasn't the impropriety that had Callie shaking in her boots. She knew Jude planned to thrash her, and judging how angry it made him that she'd annoyed the other passengers purposely, she didn't imagine it would be a few light swats. Still, he had also treated her kindly and didn't seem angry anymore, so she held out hope that he would forget his promise.

That hope was soon dashed. She watched in horror as Jude unbuckled his belt, sat down on the bed, and laid the leather strap next to him. He patted his leg. "Come lay yourself over my knee, Callie. Let's get your punishment over with." His voice was firm and held a trace of weariness. She could hear that he was worn out from the long two days in which he didn't sleep, instead maintaining focus on his driving.

She gave him a mournful look from where she stood a few paces away, clasping her hands behind her back. "Please, Jude, I'm sorry—"

"Come to me now," he interrupted, his voice taking on a hard edge. "You knew this was going to happen, and I don't want to hear any arguments."

His impatient tone caused her heart to pound, and she felt even less inclined to position herself in such a way to feel his wrath. She blinked and gaped at the belt on the bed, which she knew would light a fire on her bottom as soon as she obeyed and lay over his lap. She tried to summon the courage to step forward, but the memory of the painful spanking in the barn, combined with Jude's present foul mood, filled her with apprehension.

"Don't make me come and get you," he growled. "It'll be much worse for you if I have to."

She felt the blood pumping in her ears with every beat of her heart, and she began to tremble. Her nose burned, indicating she was moments from crying. With every ounce of courage she could summon, she walked to him. Her eyes stung with tears as he took hold of her hand. She looked into his dark eyes, which were studying her intently, and noticed them soften before he pulled her over his lap. Her arms and legs dangled in the air, while her torso spanned his thighs. She squeezed her eyes shut as he wrapped his hand around her waist to hold her in place.

"You're shaking like you've been in the snow for hours and not in the hot sun," he observed.

"I-I'm really scared," she said, the fear obvious from her wavering voice.

"You're supposed to fear punishment *before* misbehaving. The whole point of punishment is to keep you from doing something bad again. Why didn't you think of the spankings I already gave you before acting up today?"

She sniffled, already starting to cry. "I did. But at the time a spanking seemed worth being up in the seat with you, rather than sitting in the coach with folks who hate me."

"They don't hate you, Callie. You've got to give them a chance. If you're respectful toward people, they'll generally be nice to you in return."

He placed his hand on her bottom, and Callie felt something quite similar to fear but entirely more pleasant in her nether regions. The pleasure confused her.

She squirmed. "Just get it over with. I'm used to being punished. I've been punished all my life." This she said more to herself than to him in order to convince herself there was nothing to fear. Callie heard him sigh, and she clenched her bottom cheeks, waiting for the first smack.

Instead, he continued to talk to her. "You've been *mistreated* your whole life. Someone who mistreats you is different from someone who disciplines you for your own good."

His words broke something inside of her. She felt anguished, followed by a rush of anger. Anger was the only way she knew how to express the strong feelings that were bursting in short, painful spurts inside of her. "I hate you!" she told him through a sob. She hoped her outburst would make him shut up and get on with punishing her. She didn't want to talk. She didn't want to think about her feelings. They were too raw, too terrifying, and she wanted no part of them.

"No, you don't," he continued in the same tone. "You hate that I'm holding you accountable for your actions, when no one has bothered to do so before. It's new and confusing for you."

"I got thrown in a closet every time I was bad," she snapped. "You don't know what you're talking about."

"No," he argued. "You got thrown in a closet whenever you were an inconvenience. No one cared enough to discipline you to make you a better person, only to cast you out of their sight when you annoyed them. You didn't deserve that treatment. I promise you that."

"Ohh," Callie sobbed. "P-please stop talking, Jude. Please just punish me. I c-can't take this. I beg you." By this time, she wanted nothing more than to feel the bite of leather, to move the pain from something emotional to something physical.

Jude picked up the belt. She heard the buckle clink as he folded the strap in two. Then a line of fire licked over her clothed bottom, and she hissed in a breath. The next lash was even harder, but the sting felt good. She wanted more. She wanted to be thrashed hard for as long as it took to draw out the pain she felt inside. Again and again the belt kissed her upended seat, and Callie moaned, relieved as her heartache faded. When Jude stopped whipping her, she lay limply over his lap and relaxed as his hand caressed her bottom.

"Good girl," he murmured, and Callie burst into tears again, not from sadness or pain, but from something else she couldn't quite understand. How she felt in that moment, after being punished, was far different from how she felt after being thrown in the closet. Before, she had felt abandoned. Now, she felt the opposite. She felt Jude's presence quite strongly.

He pulled her up and sat her smarting bottom on his left leg. When he handed her his handkerchief, she blew her nose.

"Tell me why I punished you, darlin'."

Callie hiccupped. "Because I annoyed everyone on purpose so I could sit in the box seat."

He wrapped his arms around her and pulled her close, and she leaned her head against his chest. "That's right. And that's bad behavior, something a petulant child would do."

She sniffled and nodded, feeling very chastised like before when he punished her, but this time she also felt cared for.

"And I'll tell you how you can know this punishment was for your own good, and not because you're an inconvenience to me."

She pulled away slightly and looked at him. "How?"

His eyes twinkled. "Well, I wanted you up in the seat with me. If I didn't care about you learning to behave, I would have been happy with the result."

She gave him a small smile. "Really?"

He nodded. "Yes, really. I'm quite fond of you. Don't tell the others, but you're my favorite out of all of them. In fact, you're my favorite passenger ever."

Callie's heart swelled, and her smile broadened. She couldn't remember ever being anyone's favorite. Sam liked her. He may have even loved her, but she always knew he loved his children more.

Jude kissed her forehead and loosened his hold around her. "Let's get some sleep now. I'm dragged out, and I'm sure you are too."

Callie marveled over the chaste kiss and felt it tingling on her skin long after it was over. She stood from his lap and pulled back the coverlet. When she climbed under it, Jude tucked it around her. As she hoped he would, he lay next to her. Their bodies didn't touch, but the space between them seemed very small. She would only need to scoot over slightly to feel his chest against her back.

She let out a sigh of pleasure when his hand stroked her arm down to her hand. He took her hand in his and skimmed her knuckles with his thumb.

"Sweet little hellion," he murmured. "Giving me so much trouble. What am I going to do with you?"

His chiding made her ache and feel cherished at the same time. Jude knew her. He knew how much trouble she could be, and she had certainly been an unruly handful, and yet he seemed so very fond of her. How strange it was to be known and also liked.

He released her hand and reached up to

brush his thumb over her ear, remembering how she couldn't handle silence in the dark. His touches felt so tender, so kind. Her heart fluttered, knowing that the same hand could turn to steel if she misbehaved. She felt drawn to his strength as much as his tenderness, and she longed to feel both in that moment. She wanted him to grab her into his arms and kiss her hard. She remained still and took deep, calming breaths, afraid of the powerful feelings growing inside of her that seemed nearly impossible to contain.

After some time, his hand fell to the side, no longer providing her with the sounds of a river. She felt only a moment's panic. It dissipated when she heard a loud snore coming from the man beside her. The louder he snored, the more she smiled. As she drifted into sleep, the last thought on her mind was that if Jude were her husband, she would never have to worry about panicking in silence again. He snored like a bear, and she had never felt so calm in the dark.

CHAPTER SEVEN

The party assembled in front of the stagecoach, which was strapped to four fresh horses. Jude observed everyone and felt satisfied that they appeared well-rested. Callie looked especially bright and energetic. He'd risen early to request a bath be drawn. When he left the room, she'd scrubbed off all the grime from travel. He tried not to imagine her naked in the bath, and he tried not to notice how pretty she looked when she joined him outside. Her porcelain skin looked so soft he longed to touch it, and her green eyes sparkled under long, thick lashes.

Jude himself felt quite a bit better after his bath. It made him feel civilized. He would enjoy it while it lasted. It would be some time before they would be able to rest again like they were able to do in Paselo. The next leg of the journey was mostly desert and, while the roads weren't too rough, it would be a hot and miserable experience. He would also need to be on the lookout for Pawnee and road agents. If they struck at all, it would likely be during the next stretch.

Coming to a decision, he addressed Billy. "I want you and your gun in the box with me during this leg. I need you to watch for any trouble."

Billy agreed and climbed up to the seat. Jude looked at Callie and wasn't at all surprised by her wounded expression, which she focused on him without reservation. Her brows were pulled together in an angry frown, and he knew he would need to talk to her to make sure she behaved. He doubted she would so quickly forget the lesson he'd imparted the evening before, but a reminder wouldn't hurt.

He crooked his finger, indicating that she was to come to him. She sighed and ambled over.

"You'd better wipe that pout off your face, girl," Jude said mildly, giving her the opportunity to express her displeasure.

Predictably, she scowled at him. "I'm a good shot. You don't believe me, but I can prove it to you. Just give me your Colt for two shakes and I'll blow your mind."

"That's what I'm afraid of," was his dry response. "Besides, I want you safe in the coach. Let the menfolk be in charge of sorting things, should something happen."

When she crossed her arms and continued to glare at him, he spoke sternly. "I expect you to behave yourself, young lady. This next stretch could be dangerous, and I need you to mind me, just like I need the others to do. I know *they* will, but I'm afraid you might give me trouble. Am I right to fear that?"

Her face morphed into a look of resignation, and she uncrossed her arms. "I won't give you any trouble, Jude. But can I sit with you during the next leg?"

He nodded. "Yes. Now get in the coach. And don't be making a nuisance of yourself unless you want a repeat of last night."

She scowled once again. "I don't need to be reminded. I've got more than air under my hair."

Jude narrowed his eyes and turned her around by her shoulders. He landed a hard swat on her bottom that sent her scurrying to the coach. "Brute!" she shouted at him when she was well out of his reach.

"Brat," he shot back.

She dissolved into giggles and stepped into the coach. Her little musical laugh brought a smile to Jude's face that lasted for miles. He hadn't heard her laugh before, and he decided he liked it quite a lot. The troublesome little lady was occupying most of his thoughts lately. He sobered with that realization. He had enjoyed the company of many young female travelers throughout his five-year employment with Wells Fargo, but he'd never become so involved with one.

Jude imagined that she was quite innocent with regard to the relations between a man and woman, and he found himself wanting to teach her the pleasures to be found in her own body, just as much as he wanted to teach her to behave. It had taken every ounce of self-control not to touch her body intimately the night before. The feel of her soft hand in his had caused desire to surge through him, as had her breasts' swell with every breath.

He liked the thought of guiding her on more than just the journey west, and a sadness struck him when he realized he would only be in her company for another couple of weeks. Then she would be gone from his life forever. Callie was engaged to another man, and he needed to remember that. It bothered him, though, that he didn't know anything about her fiancé. After having such a rough go of life, he would like to know that Callie's future held at least a chance for happiness with this stranger.

During his musings, he drove the horses by habit. As he'd hoped, Billy turned out to be a fine guard. He kept an eye on the horizon for bandits and Indians and had impressive peripheral vision. At one point Billy stood, raised his gun, and aimed straight for a bush a couple hundred yards away. Jude stiffened and collected the reins more tightly in his hands, ready to either stop or gallop the horses depending on what the situation called for.

The sound of Billy chuckling made Jude relax. "Just a prairie dog." He lowered his gun and sat back down.

Jude grinned. "Seems you're the right man for the job. If your ears are half as good as your eyes, next you'll be hearing a rattlesnake from a mile away."

Billy's awareness of possible danger allowed Jude to concentrate on driving the horses and also gave him ample opportunity to think about Callie's future. He decided that he would make sure this Albert fellow was decent before he left her in his care. If her fiancé had lied about his circumstances, or if Callie was in any way displeased with him, he would take the girl back with him to St. Louis. He felt satisfied with this plan, and he relaxed some more.

That's when a gunshot exploded in the air, startling Jude, the horses, and everyone else. Jude felt fear grip him like it never had before during staging. Although he had dealt with danger multiple times on the line, the thought of something happening to Callie sent a bolt of anger and alarm right through him. Galloping hooves circled the back of the stagecoach, putting the bandit out of sight briefly. Jude brought the horses to a sharp but safe halt. Reaching for his Colt as Billy cocked his rifle, the two of them focused their weapons on the man rounding the coach.

"Drop the guns," the man snarled, a Remington pointed directly at Jude's head. "No one needs to get hurt. I'm only here for money and goods."

"You'd better hightail it out of here, agent," Jude said, his gun aimed between the man's beady black eyes. "You won't be leaving with anything but your life, unless you piss me off. There are two guns to your one. Get a move on."

Jude saw the man's eyes twinkle, though he couldn't see his smile through the red bandana over his mouth. "There may be two guns, Brother Whip, but yours is useless. It's not cocked, and it's not in your shootin' hand." His voice held a trace of amusement, as though he was dealing with an amateur. And he was. Jude's skill lay in driving, not shooting. Jude hadn't had the time to cock his weapon and transfer it from his left to right hand after stopping the horses.

The bandit continued to speak, now in a hard voice. "I don't wanna kill you, but I will, so I suggest you do as I say."

"What's to stop me from shooting you right now?" Billy asked. "Your iron's not pointed in my direction, but mine's aimed at your skull."

The bandit scoffed. "You won't shoot me if you have a lick of sense. Because if you do, I'll make sure to shoot your driver here before I die, and then you'll all die at the Lupeguad Pass without him. Lower your weapons. I won't ask politely again."

The next thing Jude heard paralyzed him with fear. It was the sound of the stagecoach door squeaking open and Callie's voice calling out.

"What's going on?" she asked in a tentative voice.

Jude's heart raced. *This can't be happening. Didn't she know not to call attention to herself?* His gaze didn't leave the bandit's face, but he saw Callie out of the corner of his eye stepping down from the coach. "Get back inside," he ordered. Jude knew what a man with loose morals might do with a vulnerable girl like Callie. If Jude got himself shot, he wouldn't be able to protect her. Anger over that realization coursed through his veins. The girl had been mistreated her whole life, and Jude wanted nothing more than to see to her safety. At the moment, however, his ability to protect her was severely compromised.

"That's my friend you're pointing your gun at, JJ," Callie said, anger in her voice.

Of all the things Jude might've thought she'd say, that would have been low on his list of possibilities. Jude and the bandit continued to stare at each other. The bandit's face contorted into a confused expression that mirrored his own feelings. A moment of confused silence hung between the men before the agent broke it.

"Callie?" the bandit said without looking at her. "Tell me that's not you."

"In the flesh," she snapped, "and like I said, that's my friend. You'd better not shoot him. I'd never forgive you."

Jude's confusion only deepened, but the bandit's seemed to end. He groaned. "I can't very well put down my weapon until your friend and his guard do. You make that happen, Miss Callie, and I'll leave your party in peace."

None of the men made any move to relieve themselves of their guns. "Well, Jude?" Callie said. "You heard him. Put down your weapon. He won't rob us."

How did Callie know this man? And how were they on what appeared to be friendly terms? Jude knew those questions would have to wait. He didn't see a better way out of the situation, so he lowered his gun and set it next to him with a silent prayer that he was making the right choice. After a slight hesitation, Billy did the same.

True to his word, the bandit shucked his Remington. "I'll be leaving then, and y'all can thank the little lady for escaping today with your tin and tricks. You're lucky I owe her a favor." He moved his horse forward. "Didn't think I'd see you again, Callie."

"Me neither. Don't you ride with a gang these days, JJ?"

He nodded once. "When I have to. But I heard tell there wasn't a guard on this here coach and thought a holdup would be as easy as lickin' butter off a knife. Didn't reckon it'd be carrying the best gunslinger since Wild Bill, or I'd've brought all the boys." With that, he laughed, neck-reined his horse, and galloped away.

Jude stared at the cloud of dust the agent left in his wake, still trying to understand what had just happened. The rest of the group seemed just as stunned, save for Callie who walked over and stood below where Jude sat. Her soft touch on his leg caused him to look down at her.

"Are you all right?" she asked, her voice barely above a whisper. Big, concerned green eyes locked with his.

He still felt too flummoxed to find the right words to form the right questions. He removed his Stetson from his head and his bandana from his pocket. Wiping his brow and neck soaked the material with his sweat.

"He's not the worst man I've ever known, but I know for a fact he's dangerous," Callie said. "I was scared. I didn't want him to hurt you."

Her wavering voice brought Jude to his senses. He swung down and collected Callie into his arms. She lay her cheek against his chest, and he ran his hand over her head down her wild blond hair.

"Jesse James?" he inquired quietly, for her ears only.

She nodded.

He gave her a squeeze. "You saved us all from being robbed or turned to buzzard food. I can't thank you enough, darlin'."

She lifted her head from his chest and looked up with a smile. He returned the smile and felt a nearly uncontrollable urge to kiss her. Her eyes sparkled, and her lips looked full and sweet. She might as well have begged him for a kiss, looking up at him like that.

Then the moment of fear he'd felt when he heard her voice after she opened the coach flashed through his memory, causing his smile to vanish. "If that bandit was a stranger, you wouldn't have left the coach, right?"

She shrugged and broke eye contact. "I don't know. If I thought I could help, I might've."

"Wrong answer," he said, raising his voice. "That was an unusual circumstance, and I can't say you did anything wrong. If God forbid this happens again, you will stay put and not call attention to yourself. Is that clear?" His voice had raised to a near bellow, and his hands tightened around her back. He stared hard into her face, and he could see her every emotion cross it, starting with surprise, then rebellion and annoyance, followed finally by submission to his will. This last expression on her face relieved him greatly, but he still insisted she speak.

"I asked you a question, Callie."

She swallowed and nodded. "It's clear, Jude. I will stay put."

"What happens if you disobey me?" His voice was stern, and he felt a twinge of guilt for speaking to her so sternly after she'd gotten him out of hot water, but the thought of her putting herself in harm's way compelled him to drive the point home.

Her eyes widened and she studied him, likely surprised that he was speaking to her this way also after the large favor. She opened her mouth. "I-I get…"

"You get what?" he growled, taking her chin in his hand firmly and forcing her to keep focus on his face.

"P-punished."

"That's right, and how will I punish you?" He knew she felt embarrassed and uncomfortable, but he didn't care. In fact, that was all the better if it would prevent her from putting herself in danger in the future.

"You'll spank me," she said in a whisper. Pink stained her cheeks, and she blinked her wide eyes rapidly.

Satisfied, he nodded and released her chin. "That's correct, and don't you forget it." He walked to the coach, where he opened the door and peered in. "You folks all right?"

The two women were fanning themselves, and the senator appeared white as a ghost. "We're fine," Annie said in a shaking voice. "Is Billy...?"

"I'm fine too," Billy said, appearing next to Jude. Annie let out a whimper of relief upon seeing her husband. Jude left them to their joyful reunion, announcing that they would be on their way in five minutes and Callie would be joining him in the box. He winked at her and was pleased to see her face break into a smile once again.

When they resumed their journey, Jude handed Callie his revolver, which she held in her lap as she watched for trouble.

Jude had many questions. "How did you come to know Jesse James? I can't picture him visiting orphans' homes in between robbing banks and murdering people."

"I snuck out of the home a lot, one of the reasons I got locked in the closet as often as I did.

I met Jesse James outside the saloon a couple years back."

Jude felt a spark of anger at the reminder that she'd often been locked in a closet without food and water. He hated the thought of her scared and alone. He also hated the thought of her wandering the streets without supervision. "Do I want to know what you were doing outside of a saloon?"

She looked at him with her wide, innocent eyes, which made his heart ache. "I went there to ask Sam for food when I was hungry. He was at the saloon most nights after his long days of rounding cattle."

"I see." The wind was picking up, causing dust to cloud around them. Jude handed Callie a clean bandana from his trousers' pocket. She wrapped the blue material around her nose and mouth. Raising her voice to continue her story, she said, "One day I went to the saloon looking for Sam, and Jesse James called to me from a hiding spot behind a barrel in the alley next to it. Of course, I didn't know it was him at the time. He said he was real hungry and asked me to fetch him some vittles. Well, I know what it's like to be hungry and in trouble, so I didn't ask questions about why he was hiding. When Sam gave me food that day, I shared it with JJ."

Jude slowed the horses to a walk as they traveled over semi-rough terrain. The wheels beneath them rattled, and the jolting added misery to an already miserable stretch of dust and wind.

"When I delivered the food, he told me he couldn't repay me with money," Callie continued, "but he said if I was interested in learning how to shoot, he would show me. So that's how he paid his debt. He gave me shooting lessons and told me I was a quick study."

Jude let out a low whistle. "I can't believe he admitted to you that he was Jesse James. Seems risky."

"Oh, he didn't tell me," Callie explained. "He told me to call him JJ. It was only after he was long gone that I saw a wanted poster with his photograph and put two and two together."

"Ah, that makes more sense."

The two of them fell into silence. He replayed the events of the day in his head and lingered on Callie's explanation of the circumstances surrounding her acquaintance with Jesse James. He had a hard time getting the thought of Callie hungry and thirsty in a dark closet out of his mind, and he also struggled to push out the image of her wandering the streets alone. These thoughts caused a powerful feeling to brew in his chest that he'd never known before. It felt similar to anger—certainly as strong as that— but unlike anger it also felt painfully tender.

Later, when they'd stopped at a swing station to sleep for the night, Jude unrolled his blanket next to Callie's. When it became dark and he heard her whimper, he understood where her fear came from. Without hesitation or concern for propriety, he pulled her into his arms and kissed her cheek. "You're not in a closet, darlin'. I've got you." He felt her body soften and relax against his. Lying there with the girl in his arms, he realized what he was feeling toward her. It could only be one thing, and it wasn't something he could easily ignore.

God dammit, Jude, he said to himself as he breathed in the floral, musky aroma of her hair. *Why'd you have to go and fall in love like a damn fool?*

CHAPTER EIGHT

Callie woke up several times during the night. Feeling a man's arms around her was new to her, and it felt so pleasant that she didn't want to miss it by sleeping. Better than pleasant, she felt safe while she lay in Jude's arms listening to his snoring, which provided a steady reminder that she was not alone. Her body felt alive. A churning in her nether regions ignited her imagination. She imagined Jude stroking her body, especially the ache between her legs that seemed to grow stronger as the night went on.

When morning came, she opened her eyes to find Jude rolling his blanket next to her. Seeing that she was awake, he smiled. "How'd you sleep?"

"Very well," she lied, yawning and sitting up.

She shyly watched him button his shirt and slide his belt around his waist. She found herself wondering if Albert was handsome like Jude. This had never concerned her before. She then felt guilty for having unwholesome thoughts about Jude. Soon she and Albert would be married, and Jude would be driving his stagecoach a thousand miles away. It wasn't right for her to feel for Jude the feelings she was meant to have for Albert.

She shook off her amorous thoughts. "You snore really loud, you know," Callie informed him as she stood and gathered the end of the blanket into her hands. She smirked at him as she rolled the material.

He regarded her for some time with a serious expression. She couldn't find a trace of amusement in his features. Crossing his arms, he said, "You snore also. In fact, before last night, I'd have wagered it wasn't possible for such loud noises to come from such a small woman."

Callie gasped, mortified. She felt warmth blooming over her cheeks and around her ears. "I do not!"

Jude's lips twitched and she saw the twinkle in his eye. He knew he'd embarrassed her and didn't hesitate to continue. "I woke up in the middle of the night, and for a moment I thought I'd wandered into a bear's cave."

She dropped her bedroll and placed her hands on her hips. "You're pulling my leg." Whether or not it was true, he had managed to embarrass her as she had tried to do to him, and she didn't like the change of events. A growl of frustration reverberated in her throat, causing Jude to laugh.

"It sounded just like that, only quite a bit louder," he told her.

"I hate you," she said, and stomped her foot.

"No, you don't," he replied, still laughing. He strode to the door and walked outside.

When they were all set to leave, Callie sat in the box seat once again. Jude seemed different during the next stretch. He didn't make much conversation with her but would often inquire into her comfort and health. Callie felt perfectly fine, but Jude said he thought she looked feverish, so he insisted that she drink half a canteen of water. She grumbled about it, but it was of no use arguing with him. Jude was a stubborn man. She felt so full of the liquid afterwards that she thought she would burst, and soon she needed to relieve herself. Jude pulled the team to a halt and stepped off the coach as she did. He made like he would follow her until Callie spun around and growled at him, "I don't need help pissing, Jude."

His brows lifted and he folded his arms. "First of all, that language is unbecoming of a lady. Second, I don't like you walking to where I can't see you. There are coyotes, Indians, and bandits around these parts."

She groaned. "None of which care to see me *relieving myself*, I imagine. I need privacy."

Jude's lips quirked up for a moment, but then he sobered and rubbed a hand along his beard in the gesture Callie now recognized as a sign that he was thinking. "If you don't want me along, I'll ask Annie to go with you."

Callie opened her mouth to protest, but he held up his hand. "It's either me or her."

When she didn't say anything, he pivoted and walked over to where the passengers were assembled, stretching out the soreness from the first few hours of the journey.

"Annie, do me a favor and join Callie, if you please. I don't want her off by herself in these parts."

"Sure thing," Annie said. She flapped the fan in front of her face and walked toward Callie wearing a warm smile.

Callie smiled upon seeing her friendly expression. She felt bad about annoying Annie and Billy with her humming a few days back, and had made efforts to talk with them. To her surprise and relief, it was just as Jude had told her. When she started treating them respectfully, they responded in kind. Annie and Callie hiked about twenty paces away from the rest of the party and Annie stayed near while Callie rounded a bush to achieve some semblance of privacy.

"You know he's sweet on you, right?" Annie said when Callie had finished.

Callie smoothed her skirt down. "Who?" she asked.

"The driver, of course, dear. Haven't you noticed the way he looks after you? He's had a soft spot for you ever since the beginning of the journey, and now he might very well be wanting to escort you to the chapel."

Callie felt shocked by Annie's assertion. She hadn't considered that Jude might be struggling with the same feelings for her as she shamefully felt toward him. She inhaled sharply. "That can't be. I'm engaged to another, and Jude is very principled."

Annie flapped the fan in front of her face. "That makes no difference. He may not act on his feelings because of that, but the fact remains that he's mighty smitten with you."

Callie shook her head, not believing what the older woman was saying. "I know he likes me all right, but he's always bossing me around and lecturing me about needing to behave. I frustrate him."

Annie threw back her head and laughed. "That's just more proof that he's in love with you, ducky. Don't you know that men are frustrated by the women they love? You frustrate him because he wants to hug and kiss you. He bosses you around because he wants to take care of you. Plus, men tend to be bossy, especially men like him." She jutted a thumb in his direction. "He's used to being in charge. Then here you come, a lady who challenges him, and he's all balled up by it. You're one of a kind, and you done tickled his fancy something fierce."

Callie looked into the distance where Jude stood, still unconvinced that Annie knew what she was talking about. If she *was* right, Callie didn't know what was to be done about it.

Annie seemed to notice her consternation. She wrapped an arm loosely around her shoulders and directed her back to the coach. "Don't fret about it. You didn't do anything wrong, you were only yourself. If you weren't already engaged, I might suggest you open yourself up to courtship —the driver seems a good man, and he makes an honest living—but as it stands, he'll just have to find himself another woman."

Callie nodded and allowed Annie to lead her back. When they reached the coach, Annie gave her hand a squeeze and returned to her seat next to Billy, while Callie stared at Jude. He set the hoof of one of the rear horses down—he always checked the horses' feet for debris when they stopped—and observed Callie, who then realized she was gaping at him. She cleared her throat and looked away.

"You all right?"

She swallowed and nodded, feeling very shy suddenly. Jude held out his hand to help her up to the box seat. When she placed her hand in his and felt it being enveloped by his callused fingers, a jolt of pleasure shot through her arm and bloomed over her body. The sensation was so powerful that she almost pulled her hand away, but instead she took a deep breath and allowed herself to be helped up the steps.

As they ambled along to the next station, Callie realized something. She hadn't read Albert's letters for two days, and her thoughts had been nearly entirely occupied by Jude. She tried, but she couldn't find the thrill she once had over her future marriage to Albert, and now she almost dreaded their arrival in Sacramento. It meant something she didn't like to think about: She'd have to say goodbye to Jude.

CHAPTER NINE

They traveled five more days, resting at small swing stations most evenings, until they reached the home station in the bustling town of Cutson, New Mexico. Jude made arrangements at the local inn for three rooms, once again putting him and Callie in a room together overnight. He didn't care about propriety when it came to that. He wouldn't leave her alone to suffer night terrors, when something as simple as holding her in his arms provided her with relief. Of course, it was uncomfortable for him. Feeling her firm young body in his arms all night without the right to stroke and touch her was a special kind of torture. The thought of never holding her in his arms again tortured him even more.

Jude felt glad to finally be at this particular town because it had a telegraph office. He often sent telegrams to his bosses alerting them of delays and providing a status on how he, the passengers, and the stagecoach fared. This time, however, he had a much different purpose for visiting.

Upon ensuring that all passengers were comfortable and well fed, he walked the dusty half-mile to the telegraph office. The bell on the door jingled as he entered, and he greeted the man wearing a green visor at the counter. "Hello, Walt. How's tricks?"

"Oh, not too tricky," Walt said. "Your travels going all right?"

"Can't complain," Jude responded. They had this exact conversation every time Jude stopped by. His next words, however, were new. "I need to send a telegram to the marshal in Sacramento."

Walt's eyebrows shot up. "You experiencing trouble of some sort?"

"No, no," Jude said impatiently, not wishing to discuss his motives. "Nothing like that. I've just got a general question about a man who lives there."

Walt nodded and handed him a pencil and paper. "You know the drill. Twenty-five cents for ten words."

Jude wrote his message on the slip of paper. He'd already penned it in his head.

I respectfully inquire into the age and financial circumstances of a certain Albert Smith <stop> Miner and resident of Sacramento <stop> Direct response to Angelos City <stop> Driver Jude Johnson <stop> Wells Fargo

As Jude handed three quarters to Walt, he thought about how truly difficult life could be for a young woman like Callie, without means to send a simple inquiry. If she'd had the money, she might have gained important information before setting out on her journey, enough to prevent her from making a horrible mistake. His heart constricted painfully at the thought of her marrying someone who didn't deserve her or, even worse, someone who mistreated her. In addition to whatever information the marshal provided, Jude fully intended to discover everything there was to know about Albert Smith upon their arrival in Sacramento. If anything was amiss, he would see to it that Callie didn't go through with the wedding.

❅ ❅ ❅

Callie turned up the oil lamp and slipped into bed. It was dark but for the low light. Jude hadn't yet returned from an errand he said he must attend to, and she found herself unable to sleep and yearning for him to be in bed with her. She thought about the progression of her friendship with Jude. Never had she felt so safe and content as the nights when Jude held her. Although she had teased him about his snoring, it brought tremendous comfort to her. She wondered if Albert snored. Would it feel as good to lie in bed with his arms around her?

She didn't particularly want to think about that, so her mind wandered back to thoughts of Jude. She imagined lying over his lap naked while his hand stroked the length of her body, from the nape of her neck down to her bottom and backs of her thighs. The spankings he'd given her had hurt at the time, but she liked remembering and fantasizing about them. Jude looked handsome even when he was angry—perhaps especially then. His dark eyes flashed and his firm jaw became impossibly harder. Then there was his voice when he scolded her before and during a spanking. It was deep and serious, yet still gentle, leaving her feeling both contrite and cared for at the same time.

She ran her hand up her inner thighs and squeezed her eyes shut as she imagined what would happen if she lost her temper and told Jude she hated him again. He would surely spank her bare bottom.

"That's it!" he would declare, peeling off his suede driving gloves and slapping them on the table. Her mind's eye watched him cross the room to the bed with thunderous strides. He sat down and crooked his finger. "Come here, young lady. It's time for that spanking I promised you." His voice was stern, but she saw a twinkle in his eye.

She took slow steps in his direction. His hands looked so big, each one splayed over a denim-clad knee. Standing in front of him, she gazed at him sorrowfully and covered her behind with her palms. "I didn't mean it, Jude. Are you going to spank me hard?"

One of his giant hands wrapped around her arm and pulled her into that vulnerable position over his lap. When settled, her fluttering tummy pressed against his thigh, and she gasped as he slipped her drawers off her bottom and slid them down her legs. Landing a firm swat across both naked cheeks, he said, "Only as hard as you deserve." His hand descended, again and again, and the sound of bare flesh being struck by a determined palm echoed in her ears.

The spanking would sting, and the sting would become more intense the longer he kept at it. She would try to wiggle away, but a hand anchored around her waist would prevent her from doing so.

"How would you like it if I said I hated you, hmm?" he scolded, smacking each cheek harder.

"I wouldn't like it one bit, Jude. I'm sorry! I'll never say it again."

"No, you won't," he agreed, and maneuvered his punishing hand to her thighs to land a few sound swats on each one. "Otherwise, you'll be right back over my knee for another spanking on this naughty bottom of yours. Understand?"

"Yes, Jude." She fantasized that she felt meek from the chastisement and longed for him to be pleased with her again.

With one final swat, the punishment ended. His hand loosened from around her waist, and he massaged her lower back with his thumb, while the callused fingers of his other hand trailed up and down each burning globe. "What happens when you misbehave, eh, Callie?"

"You spank me."

She realized she said those words out loud in the empty hotel room, and her face heated. Her breathing was shallow and she became aware of a pulsing between her legs. Imagining it was Jude's hand stroking between her legs while she lay sprawled over his lap after punishment, she dipped her hand under her drawers and slipped two fingers between the slick folds of her womanhood. Gasping when she flicked her sensitive nub, she focused on that spot and rubbed with vigor, all the while pretending that it was Jude touching her intimately.

Unaware of anything but the pleasure, she didn't hear the door of the hotel room open. As the wave of warmth caused her body to spasm and her back to arch, she caught Jude's movement out of the corner of her eye. She locked eyes with him and screamed, both from mortification and from her release.

Beyond embarrassed and afraid of what he might think of her, she threw the quilt over her face and remained silent, hoping he would forget what he'd just walked in on and not breathe a word of it. Of course, that was not to be.

"I'm sorry to interrupt," he said wryly.

She moaned. Her voice muffled by the quilt, she said, "Please forget what you saw, Jude."

"I heard it more than I saw it." She detected amusement in his voice, though she could tell he was trying to sound stern. "That's very naughty behavior. Tell me, who were you thinking of while you pleasured yourself in that way? Me?"

The tease in his voice infuriated her, as did his presumptiveness. "Of course not! I would never! How could you even think that?" she shouted from underneath her blanket.

He laughed. "There's a saying I learned in school, something about how the lady doth protest too much."

Callie pushed the quilt away from her face and glared at him. "How did you know I was thinking of you?" she demanded.

Jude's eyes widened with surprise. He coughed in an attempt to muffle a laugh and raked his fingers through his hair. "Criminy, Callie. I didn't, until just now." He walked to the basin on the dresser across the room from the bed, where he washed his hands and splashed water on his face.

Callie groaned when she realized that she'd just shared way more than she should have. She watched him lie on the floor next to the bed. He reclined on his back and covered his face with the crook of his elbow as though he couldn't bear to look at her.

Callie felt miserable. "Do you think less of

me, Jude? Do you think I'm a wanton woman?"

"No," he said gruffly. "Go to sleep."

She didn't believe him, and there was no way she could sleep. "If you don't think less of me, why are you lying on the floor instead of holding me like you've been doing up to now?"

"Because I'm a man," he responded, as though that answered the question.

When the silence that followed made it clear he wasn't going to expound on that explanation, she spoke again. "But I don't understand," she said, raising her voice with emotion. "What does that have to do with anything?"

Jude removed his arm from his face and looked over at her with a strange intensity in his eyes. "If I lie in bed with you, I'll want to give you more pleasure and also derive pleasure from you. It's not proper for unmarried folks, and I don't want to take advantage. Surely you're not so innocent that you can't understand that."

His words caused her longing and ache to resume. "You want to touch me? Down there?" she asked breathily.

He groaned and looked at the ceiling. "Please go to sleep, Callie."

It was unusual for him to request something from her without ordering it. It almost sounded like he was begging her, and she felt disconcerted as well as embarrassed. She sighed, not tired in the least, and gazed at the flame of the lamp until it flickered out.

The darkness that suddenly surrounded her crowded out her concern and embarrassment. She felt the familiar rise of panic, which pooled in her throat and led to a wave of nausea. Jude hadn't fallen asleep. She knew this because he wasn't snoring. If he had been, she might have been able to contain the panic. Reverting to how she coped before meeting Jude, she began to hum. It didn't calm her nearly as much as when Jude held her, but it kept the panic from growing to a point where she felt she might scream.

Callie heard Jude stirring, so she stopped humming.

"Callie," he said softly. "I've changed my mind. I'm going to join you in bed, so don't be startled."

She felt the bed depress and soon after, her back was tucked into his chest and his arms were around her. A wave of happiness and relief washed over her. He didn't think badly of her after all. "What made you change your mind?"

He brushed some of her hair aside and kissed the shell of her ear. His kiss caused her skin to tingle and her ache between her legs to pulse. She pressed into him harder, needing to feel as much of him as possible.

"I can't bear to know you're scared. I want to make you feel safe."

His simple statement brought her comfort and caused her to remember what Annie had told her. Maybe Jude really *was* sweet on her. If so, would he propose that she marry him instead of Albert? She hoped so, but after thinking on it, she knew he wouldn't. Not in a million years. Jude wouldn't think it proper to break up her engagement with another man. She recalled Jude's words, which as much as guaranteed he wouldn't act on any feelings he might have for her. *When it's hardest to be a good person, that's when it's most important.*

* * *

As the days passed, Jude noticed that the passengers had come to like Callie, except for the senator, who still regarded her with disdain. Even the senator's wife had softened considerably toward the girl. On one of their stops, Jude walked with Callie for a spell, chatting and enjoying her company. Callie had been spending time with the others in the coach, while Annie had joined him in the box, and he missed talking to her. He knew he should get used to being without her company, since he would be saying goodbye to her soon, but he didn't want to think about that.

By this time, Callie was agreeable to sharing the box seat and didn't behave sullenly about it. "I'm real proud of you for having a good attitude, darlin'," he told her. "Seems like you grew from a child to a woman right before my eyes."

She shrugged, seeming uncomfortable by

his praise. "I don't want another spanking. You pack a hard wallop."

He chuckled. "If it's fear of punishment that keeps you on the straight and narrow, so be it, although I hope someday you'll actually *want* to behave properly."

She glanced over at him and smiled. "I do want to behave, Jude. I also want to make you happy. I've thought a lot about what you've told me, about keeping my word and treating people with respect."

He smiled back at her. "I can see that. You're a fine lady, Callie. Plus you're smart as a whip and cute as a button."

She laughed her little musical laugh. "My goodness, Jude," Callie said in a teasing voice. "So many compliments. If I didn't know better, I'd say you were sweet on me."

Her eyes seemed to linger on his face for longer than normal after making that statement. Jude stared back at her, unsure of what to say. He thought about confessing to her right then and there that he was indeed sweet on her, but he decided against it. There was no point in her knowing. He had lectured Callie about how it was wrong to steal. Stealing another man's woman would make him the world's greatest hypocrite, and he'd already decided he would only whisk Callie away if her intended wasn't who he said he was.

He changed the subject. "Are you getting

along all right with Senator Tucker?"

"Yes," she said, sobering. "He still hates me though."

Jude figured as much, and wasn't happy with the news, but he reckoned there wasn't much he could do about it. However, a couple of days later, he wished he had spoken with the senator and warned him against doing anything malicious toward Callie. An admonishment might have stopped him from stealing and getting rid of her only belongings—the suede pouch, her mother's brooch, Sam's lucky penny, and the letters from Albert. Of course, no one could prove that the senator had stolen Callie's things, but no one had any doubts about who had done it either. It was a hurtful move that unsettled everyone and devastated Callie.

They had stopped briefly to rest the horses, and Jude was first alerted to the problem when he heard Callie's anguished cry. "I have to find it!"

"All right, dear, all right. Let me help you look," Annie said. "It must be here somewhere." She lifted the shawl that laid across one of the coach seats.

"It's not anywhere in the coach," Callie said, her voice rising in a panic. "I already looked."

Jude walked over and joined Annie in her search for the satchel, just to double-check. They looked over every inch of the coach and checked the few nooks and crannies more than once. Jude had a horrible suspicion about what happened, but he desperately hoped he was wrong. He rubbed the back of his neck. "Do you reckon you left it at the last station?"

"No, Jude. I always keep it tied to me! It must have been stolen while I dozed off during the last stretch." She turned accusing eyes on the senator, who was leaning casually against the coach, observing the scene.

"I know you took it," she said in a low, trembling voice.

The senator's face twisted into a mean smirk. "Just because you're inclined to steal doesn't mean the rest of us are."

Callie raised her voice. "I gave your watch back. I did the right thing!"

Jude's spirits were low. He guessed that the senator had not only stolen Callie's pouch, he'd also ditched it somewhere behind them on the line. "Look, Senator, if you were meaning to teach Callie a lesson, you've made your point. Give the pouch back to her now."

The senator focused his contemptuous gaze on Jude. His next words confirmed Jude's fear. "Let's suppose for a minute that I did take the girl's worthless belongings off her hands. You really think I'd still have them? I'd rather hold on to a mangy mutt than keep her stinking satchel near my person."

"That was everything I owned in the world!" Callie shouted. Her voice shook with fury. "You'd better watch your back, you shit-eating, miserly old sycher. I swear I'll slit your throat in your sleep."

Mrs. Tucker gasped and Annie held the back of her hand to her forehead. "Sakes alive." Billy looked incredibly uncomfortable. Jude doubted Billy had ever heard such language outside of a saloon, and he was reasonably certain the ladies hadn't ever heard those words spoken aloud anywhere.

"That's enough, Callie," Jude said sternly.

"I'll saw off your dick and feed it to the coyotes," she continued, tears streaming down her face. "You'll be sorry, you bastard. I'll make you so sorry."

Callie was growing more hysterical. Jude reached out and took hold of her arm. He needed to get her away from the other passengers and calm her down. "I'm just going to have a talk with Callie. We'll be on our way in a few minutes," he informed the others. He led Callie around the corner.

She struggled to free herself from his grasp. "Let me go, Jude!"

"I will, darlin', but you need to calm down." He led her to a private area behind a thick group of trees before he stopped and released her. As soon as he let go, she dashed away from him with surprising speed.

"Stop right now, Callie," he said loudly, striding after her. "If I have to run to catch you, you're going to be very sorry when I do."

His words fell on deaf ears. Callie continued

to run, so Jude broke into a jog after her. It took longer than he thought it would to catch her, and by the time he did, they were both breathing hard. Jude wrapped an arm around Callie's middle and lifted her clear off the ground. She struggled violently as he walked in the direction from which they'd come. He hefted her over his shoulder like a burden of goods to make the walk a bit easier. The difference was that this particular burden saw fit to pound her fists against his back and fling a string of obscenities at him. When she launched into an unflattering description of his mother, he finally stopped at an overturned log, where he sat and quickly maneuvered her over his lap.

Without delay, he landed a hard smack across her wriggling bottom. "I'm going to spank you until you calm down. It's up to you how long it takes," he informed her, then fell into silence and focused on his task with great attention. He smacked her crisply across both cheeks over and over, while she wailed and cursed and struggled to free herself from his iron grip on her waist. His forearm effectively pinned her to his left leg, and when she wouldn't stop kicking, he wrapped his other leg over hers, trapping her completely and allowing him to keep his target steady. After a good twenty swats or so, she stopped cursing and hung limply over his lap, sniffling quietly.

As soon as he felt her body relax, he stopped spanking and rubbed her back, murmuring comforting words as they came to him. His sympathy only seemed to make her cry more, although by this time her crying wasn't hysterical; instead it was sad and resigned. He sat her upright on his lap and hugged her to him, kissing her forehead and rubbing her back.

"Shh, darlin'. I'll buy you another satchel, and Albert will write more letters. Your mother's brooch and Sam's lucky penny? Now I know those can't be replaced and I'm sorry about that, but your ma and Sam will always be in your memory. No one can steal your memories." He handed her a bandana as a handkerchief.

She took it and blew her nose, then gazed sadly into his eyes. "I guess I deserved it after stealing his watch."

Jude smoothed some of her tangled hair behind her ear. "You didn't deserve it, honey. You deserve good things to happen to you. That's what I want for you, so much."

Her eyes were rimmed with red, and he saw a flash of fear cross them. "I'm scared, Jude. I know it sounds silly, but my lucky penny from Sam made me feel like I wasn't alone. What if Albert doesn't like me? I'll be stuck in Sacramento without a friend."

"No, honey. That's not going to happen," Jude said. "You can bet your britches I'll be making sure this Albert Smith is perfect, or just barely shy of it. And I'll make sure he's smart enough to know what a prize he has in you. Otherwise, I won't be leaving you."

Her bloodshot green eyes studied his carefully. "You'll take me back to St. Louis?"

He didn't want to get into the particulars of his desire to settle down with her. It all depended on the man Albert Smith, and it pained him to think of what might not be. "Or I'll take you somewhere else. But let's not talk about it. All you need to know is that I won't abandon you if something isn't right in Sacramento."

She rested her head on his shoulder. "Thank you, Jude. You've been so good to me."

He gave her back an affectionate rub. They were more familiar with each other than what was proper, and yet he wanted so much more. He desired nothing more than to make her his wife and hold her in his arms every night.

A few days later, when they reached their stop in Angelos City, Jude got the party situated in the hotel and walked very slowly to the telegraph office. Never had he been so nervous to receive a message. With every fiber in his being, he hoped that the marshal's report on Albert Smith was unfavorable. He wished the man to be forty years old at the youngest, dirt poor, and with a drinking problem. If he had served jail time, all the better.

Jude's normally very steady hand trembled when he picked up the envelope that held the message from Sacramento's marshal. The noise around him from pedestrians and horses felt distracting, so Jude walked away from the hustle and bustle until the noise became little more than a hum. He sat on a tree stump and took a deep breath. He carefully tore the side of the envelope and drew out the slip of paper from inside.

Albert Smith 32 years <stop> *Wealthy landowner and miner on the city council* <stop> *Regards from Marshal Gregory*

Jude's wrist slackened and he held the paper loosely in his hand. The breeze caused it to flap, a painful reminder of its presence and what it represented. Disappointment rested heavily on his shoulders. Judging by the words of the message, Albert Smith seemed to be a decent man, and Jude wouldn't be able to propose to Callie in good conscience.

Fighting off his baser feelings, he found comfort in the knowledge that she would surely have a good life as a rich miner's wife, and Albert would likely treat her well, since he was upstanding enough to serve on the voluntary city council. Though his hopes were dashed, he felt glad that Callie had a chance for happiness after the misfortune she'd experienced growing up. His gratefulness over that melded with melancholy. He knew how very much he loved her. It was enough to lose her if that was what was best for her.

CHAPTER TEN

Callie mopped her face with a bandana. It was a sweltering hot day, and she desperately needed a bath. All of travelers did, but they would arrive at their destination city dirty and sweaty. She didn't care all that much, though she knew she should, since she was hours away from meeting her future husband. Her mind was occupied with Jude, who also looked like he could use a good bath. For the last seventy miles, they talked easily with each other in the box seat. The longer they talked, the sadder Callie felt. She never wanted to be without Jude's company. She wanted him to continue to guide and enlighten her, and she wanted to continue to charm him, which she could tell she did quite well by the way his eyes danced and his mustache twitched in amusement over the things she said.

The two of them fell into silence as the outline of the city buildings came into view against the sunset. According to Jude, her future husband would likely be waiting at their stop, as Jude had sent a telegram a couple of days ago to the home station, alerting the marshal and other city officials of their arrival and listing each passenger's name. Callie tried to muster up some excitement and the will to smooth down her hair and try to look presentable, but all she felt was a sinking, sad feeling in her gut. She looked over at Jude. "So you won't leave me here if I don't want you to, right, Jude?" She needed to hear his promise once again.

He shook his head as he urged the horses forward. "No need to fret about that. I'm going to be in town for a few days anyway, looking into some things."

Jude blew the bugle, signaling to the passengers in the coach that they were minutes from the final station, which elicited whoops and hollers. It had been a long journey, and they were finally home.

Callie held up her hand to shade her eyes from the sun and peered into the small crowd of people who stood around the station. When she caught sight of a tall blond man leaning against a beam with a hand on his hip, her breath caught in her throat. She knew it was Albert. She could tell by the description he gave of himself, though he hadn't sent a photograph. As the coach came to a stop, she locked eyes with him. He gave her a small smile, then stepped forward. Her heartbeat quickened as he approached. Her fiancé was quite good-looking, and he had dressed up for the occasion with a starched white shirt and western-style bow tie. His vest was rich suede that reminded her of her suede pouch that the senator had stolen.

Callie knew she looked a fright, especially compared to him, so when he held out his hand to assist her descent, she smiled shyly and apologized. "Please excuse my appearance, Mr. Smith. I wish I could have freshened up before meeting you."

He waited until she reached the ground before speaking. His voice was polite. "Please call me Albert as you've been doing in letters, Callie. You've traveled long and hard. There's no need to apologize. I've arranged for you to stay the night in the hotel a few blocks down, where you can bathe and get a good night's sleep."

"Thank you," she said, although she worried how she would fare alone in a hotel room. It was to be expected, though. Albert wouldn't sleep in the same room with her until they were married. He was a gentleman.

"I'll fetch your luggage. Is it in the boot?"

Callie felt her cheeks grow warm. Her mind raced, assembling the lies she'd told Albert in her letters. He thought she was well off, and here she stood in a dirty torn dress with no luggage.

"I'm afraid I only have what I'm wearing." She lowered her voice so that only Albert could hear her. "The rest was stolen in a holdup. A bandit took off with my huge satchel but left everyone else's. He probably didn't want to weigh the horse down with other people's things in addition to mine." She held her breath, hopeful that he believed her.

"I'm glad you escaped unharmed when the bandit stole your things!" he exclaimed loudly.

Callie cringed and looked at Jude, who rolled his eyes and shook his head at her. Unaware of her discomfort, Albert continued, "Tomorrow I will buy you whatever supplies you might need before we get married. The ceremony will take place at sundown."

"Thank you," Callie said again, her voice barely above a whisper. She felt her heartbeat quicken over his mention of their impending marriage. "You are ever so kind."

Her friend Annie hustled over and gave her a big hug. "You take care, dear, but this isn't goodbye. I'll be looking you up after we're all settled."

Callie bid her, Billy, and the Tuckers farewell. All but the senator assured her they would be in touch. When Albert held out his bent arm, she wrapped her dirty hand around the crook of his elbow. She glanced up at Jude, who still sat in the box seat studying her and Albert carefully. She wanted more than anything to run back to him. She wanted to feel his arms around her one last time. Instead, she tore her gaze away and held on to the stranger's arm, the man she'd longed to meet for nearly a year before meeting Jude, and walked with him to the hotel.

After Albert bid her a polite goodbye and

she was left alone to bathe, she curled up in the warm water and mourned her loss. Jude would never again hold her during her night terrors. He wouldn't tease her or joke with her. He wouldn't study her with that gaze that melted the walls of lies and tall tales she used to make herself seem important. Jude was the only person who not only knew the real her, but also liked what he discovered. To experience that and then to lose it felt devastating.

Callie finished with her bath and toweled herself dry. She donned her drawers and chemise even though they were quite dirty. She had nothing else to sleep in, and it didn't feel right to sleep naked. She turned up the light from the oil lamp as high as it would go and crawled into bed, where she stared at the flickering flame, praying she would find sleep before the light went out. She was not so lucky, however. When the flame died, she trembled and began to hum, tears streaming down her face. The memory of the nights alone in the closet tortured her with a vengeance. The panic was especially bad this time, and soon she was screaming.

She heard a knock that startled her out of her terrified state. Worried that someone had come to yell at her for screaming, she tiptoed to the door and pressed her ear against it. "Who's there?" she asked.

"It's me, Callie. May I come in?"

At the sound of Jude's voice, Callie burst into

relieved tears. She opened the door and fell into his arms, never happier to see someone in all her life.

"Oh, darlin'," he said, sighing. "I was afraid of this." He swept her trembling, scantily clad body into his arms and walked in the room with her, shutting the door behind him with his boot. He carried her to the bed and set her down, then pulled up the quilt over her. "Hush, now. There's no need to cry or be afraid." He walked to the lamp and added more oil, then lit the small flame.

"I'm so happy to see you, Jude," she said through her tears. "I need you."

He returned to the bed and sat on it, then wrestled the boots off his feet and placed them aside along with his Stetson. He regarded her for a brief moment, looking conflicted, but then seemed to come to a decision. He lay next to her fully dressed and gathered her into his arms in the familiar cuddle that brought her such comfort.

"You don't need me, honey, you only think you do. You're going to be just fine." He stroked her freshly washed hair away from where it clung to her damp cheeks.

Callie didn't know what to say to that. She disagreed, but she didn't want to argue. Her feelings about the subject didn't matter. Even if Jude loved her, he wouldn't steal her from her fiancé. And if she confessed her love to him, she would be going against everything he'd taught her about being true to her word. He knew she'd promised Albert that she would marry him.

"It's very improper for me to be holding you like this, Callie," Jude said in a mournful voice. "It's your husband's pleasure to hold you, so it will be the last time that I do. Albert seems like a decent fellow. You will have a good life with him, I reckon."

Callie feared she would weep if she responded, so she stayed quiet but for a shuddering breath. It was then that she understood that Jude had come to say goodbye to her. She couldn't recall ever feeling so sad as she did in that moment, resting in his comforting arms, knowing it was the last time that she would. Jude seemed to understand what she was feeling. He hugged her tighter and buried his face in the hair cascading over the nape of her neck. He breathed in deeply and sighed.

"Will you come to the wedding, Jude?"

It took him a very long time to respond. If she didn't know how loudly he snored, she would have thought he'd fallen asleep. "I don't know if that's a good idea, honey," he said finally.

"I understand," she whispered. And she did. There was no way he'd be able to endure the pain of watching her get married if he felt anywhere near as bad about losing her as she did about losing him.

❊ ❊ ❊

When Callie woke up, Jude was gone. Judging by the bright light streaming into the window, so was most of the morning. She quickly rose from bed, washed her face, and tried without much success to dust off the dirt on her dress. It needed to be washed thoroughly over a washboard with soap and water. She walked down the steps to the front desk, unsure of what she was supposed to do first.

The innkeeper spotted her. "Miss Caroline Broderick?"

She nodded. "Yes, sir, that's me."

He walked over and handed her a note. "From Mr. Albert Smith," he explained.

Callie thanked him and meandered over to a chair by the door, where she sat and opened the envelope. She drew out the letter and unfolded it. The letter was written in Albert's familiar hand.

Dear Callie,

I hope you feel well rested after your long journey. I've made arrangements with the seamstress to supply you with two dresses, one for everyday use and a more formal one for our wedding and for church. Please also pick out whatever else you might need—shoes, stockings, etc. You'll find the dress shop three blocks east of the hotel. When you've made your selections, please join me at the diner for lunch, where we will get to know each other a bit more.

Sincerely,

Albert

Callie's eyes lingered on the word 'sincerely.' She'd never read that closing in any of his other letters to her. They were always signed 'warmly' or even 'with love.' His use of 'sincerely' seemed much stiffer. She shrugged. It was a silly thing to read into. It was clear that Albert was exactly the kind of man any sane woman would want for a husband—considerate, well-off, and handsome to boot. She recalled the many hours she'd spent reading his letters over the last nine months, imagining him and their life together. She tried to summon even a smidgen of the same excitement she once felt. Here she was, only hours from her wedding and the start of a stable, good life—what she'd been wishing for and dreaming of for so long—and she felt nothing but sorrow.

Callie found some pleasure in picking out her clothes. She'd never before owned brand-new duds. She chose a blue gingham dress with eyelet stitched around the wrists and hem of the skirt. For her more formal wear, she chose a cream-colored satin dress with black lace at the collar and delicate crystal buttons down the back. The seamstress offered to fix her hair, which was clean from the bath the night before but as unruly as ever.

Callie donned the satin dress and stood before the mirror, marveling at her appearance. Her hair was pinned in an elaborate bun on the top of her head, with soft ringlets let loose that framed her face. The curves of her slim figure were highly accentuated by the satin material. She looked like the real lady she'd pretended to be in her letters to Albert, not the scrappy girl she felt like inside.

After thanking the seamstress, Callie moseyed on over to the diner. Along the way, she took in the sights of what would be her new home. The city bustled. It was much more energetic than St. Louis, with more people. Men and women alike nodded to her and smiled pleasantly. This had never happened to her before. She'd always walked with her eyes downcast in town, afraid of being spotted. Now she walked with her head held high, like someone who belonged. It felt right, being in Sacramento. She would get used to the man she would marry, she told herself, and all would work out well. She tried to squelch the dark sadness that threatened to bubble up and smother the brief hope she'd managed to find.

She stepped into the diner and spotted Albert across the room. Upon seeing her, he set down his cup of coffee, rose, and walked toward her. She held out her hand to him. "Good afternoon, Albert."

"Hello, Callie. You look very lovely in your new dress." He kissed her hand. A man had never kissed her hand before, and she decided she liked it. She felt even more like a lady and stood a little straighter.

"Come and sit down." Albert placed his palm on her back to guide her toward the table. He held out her chair and she sat awkwardly. After he sat down across from her, he asked what she would like to eat. She felt nervous and afraid of giving him the wrong answer. What would a lady eat?

"I'll have whatever you're having, just less of it," Callie said. Her cheeks grew warm and she scolded herself. *Such a silly thing to say!*

But Albert didn't seem to think anything was amiss in her answer. He summoned the waiter and ordered her a biscuit, a slice of ham, and an egg. He then folded his hands in front of him on the table and studied her. "So, Callie, here we are." He wore a blank expression, and Callie couldn't tell if he was pleased with her or disappointed, so she felt even more nervous.

"Thank you for the dresses, Albert. You are very generous."

"You're welcome."

A silence followed, during which he continued to regard her. She couldn't be sure, but he looked sad to her, and her worry that she was a disappointment to him continued to grow. She cleared her throat. "I like this dress because it reminds me of a dress that Ophelia wore in *Hamlet*. Delightful play."

Albert took a sip of his coffee and frowned thoughtfully. "Is that right?"

She nodded. "Yes, and the day after we attended the theater, my father bought me a lovely silk scarf like Ophelia wore. It was the color of the sky just before a storm, a pretty greenish gray."

He placed his coffee cup on the table and studied her. "I'm surprised you wanted to leave what seems to have been a fine life in St. Louis and journey all the way here to an unknown future."

Callie blinked. He made a good point, and she hadn't thought that he might question her reason for moving west. She looked down, feeling ashamed, and spoke honestly. "What's the use of fine things in life, if there's no love?" She bit her lip, and tears threatened to spill. She stared at the light reflecting off her glass of water on the table, unable to meet his eyes.

Albert touched her hand. "It looks as though I've upset you. I didn't mean to. I am only trying to get to know you, and I don't mean to question your motives. Rest assured that I will marry you regardless of what brought you here or what you left behind." His voice was firm and held resolve. It wasn't the most romantic thing for him to say, but to Callie it showed that he had good character, just like Jude. It also hinted at him figuring out she wasn't quite as well off as she'd pretended to be in her letters.

She looked at him tentatively through her lashes, and he offered her a smile. The smile seemed forced, though, and Callie still felt worried that she was a disappointment to him.

"I keep my promises too," she said softly. "And from now on I want to be totally honest with you, Albert."

"I'm glad to hear that, Callie," he responded, and the smile he gave her then seemed genuine and kind.

Their conversation turned to lighter subjects, and they spoke more easily during the next hour. Although Callie continued to feel on edge, she managed to hide her apprehension. She even managed to make Albert laugh a couple times. Two things became clear to Callie by the end of their conversation. One, he was a good man and would make a fine husband. Two, it would take a lot more than that for her to forget about Jude.

❊ ❊ ❊

For most of the morning, Jude visited every establishment on Main Street inquiring into the character of Albert Smith. No one had a bad word to say about the man.

"Oh, he's a fine member. Always pays his bills on time," said the banker.

"He tells my grandmother she looks mighty

pretty whenever he stops by," said the shopkeeper.

"He's donated money to every charity and fundraiser since I've been here," said the preacher.

By noontime, Jude was thoroughly disgusted by Albert's righteousness. There was no way he could propose to her in good conscience. Still, his jaw clenched as he witnessed them exiting the diner and Albert stooping to kiss Callie's cheek. Jude studied her reaction carefully. As soon as Albert turned his back to leave, her body slumped, as though she could finally relax. He considered crossing the street to speak with her but decided against it. No good would come from spending time with her at this point.

Jude walked along the sidewalk toward the saloon. He needed a stiff drink and loud music to get his mind off of things. He strode through the double doors and sat on the only free stool at the bar, which was next to two men who appeared deep in conversation. Jude wasn't feeling social and hoped no one would try to talk to him.

"Whiskey," he ordered gruffly from the barkeep, who was a new face to him. Jude wondered absently what had happened to the man who usually tended the bar, but he didn't feel curious enough to ask. As soon as the whiskey was placed in front of him, Jude downed it. Slamming it on the bar, he growled, "Another."

This he repeated three more times, until he was well on his way to being drunk. It brought him very little relief. Hunched over his fifth whiskey, he stared at his tanned, work-weathered hands and mused about the trip. Never would he have guessed that he'd fall in love. If he had predicted its possibility, he would have been more careful during his interactions with the girl. He wouldn't have spanked her, hugged her, or engaged in long conversations with her. From the beginning, he'd thought she was cute, a fun distraction from his main focus of driving. But now, she took up all his thoughts and everything else seemed a distraction.

A long time passed, during which Jude remained seated at the bar, trying not to think about Callie but never able to get her out of his mind for longer than a few minutes. He intended to sit there until dark, when he'd know Albert and Callie's wedding was over, and then he would go drown his sorrows in his hotel room with a bottle.

Dimly, he became aware of the man seated next to him raising his voice angrily in the direction of the man sitting on the other side of him. "Can you believe that?" the stranger said, then scoffed in disgust. "I mean, I understand principles and all, but as far as I'm concerned, the promise to marry don't mean a thing until you both say 'I do.'"

"Albert's as honest as the day is long," the other man said in a conciliatory tone. "Kept every promise he ever made, I reckon."

Hearing Albert's name piqued Jude's interest. He strained his ears to hear more of the conversation.

"Honest is one thing, but he's plain pigheaded. He don't owe that girl a damn thing."

His friend took a drink from his beer glass. "Maybe not, but if he said he was going to marry her, you can be sure as a gun that's what he's gonna do, even if he don't want to. She did leave her home and travel all the way here at his beckoning."

Jude gave his head a quick shake, trying to focus. "Excuse me," he said to the irate man sitting next to him. "You aren't by any chance talking about Albert Smith, are you?"

The man glared at him and snarled, "What's it to you, mister?"

"The way you're talking, it sounds as if he doesn't want to get married."

"You heard right," he responded, scowling. "I'll repeat, what's it to you?"

Dumbfounded, it took a moment for Jude to find his tongue. "I'm a friend of the girl he's supposed to marry. Why doesn't he want to marry her? She's a fine lady." He felt his temper flare. Did Albert not think her good enough for him?

The man continued to scowl. "Don't worry, he's going to follow through on his promise. Trouble is, my daughter went to work for him a month ago and ended up falling in love with his sorry ass, and I'd bet all the whiskey in this bar that he's in love with her too." He shook his head and mumbled in the direction of the bar surface, "Damn fool."

Jude's mind raced, processing the information he'd just learned. He jumped up from his seat and looked outside. It was already growing dark. "We've got to stop this wedding," he said urgently. "That girl he's marrying is in love with me and I with her, and I'm a damn fool too."

"What in tarnation?" The man stared at Jude, shocked, while the man on the other side of him broke into loud guffaws.

"What a stupid lot we humans are," he said, laughing.

"Let's go," Jude said. He threw a wad of cash on the bar and made a beeline for the door, with the man quick at his heels.

They rushed out of the saloon and headed toward the chapel. Along the way, Jude's new friend tore into a boardinghouse and fetched his daughter, a pretty young thing whose face was streaked with tears. "I don't have time to explain, Sara, but come along to the chapel." She fell into step with them.

The church bells rang, causing Jude's step to quicken even more and his heart to race faster. The wedding had either just begun or just ended.

An unusually large number of people loitered in the streets, and they formed a thick barrier. "What's with all the people?" Jude asked, frustrated and consumed with anxiety over the delay.

"Social bee," the man muttered. "Blast it all."

"Excuse me," Jude said to a tightly assembled

group of ladies as he shoved his way through. He winced a little, knowing he was being rude, but getting to his destination in time was so important that he didn't care all that much.

"What's going on, Papa?" Sara said, out of breath from hustling. Her face was flushed and she grasped her skirts in her fists to enable her to jog along with the men. "Why are we going to Albert's wedding?"

"Because you should be marrying him, not the other girl."

Sara wailed, sounding every bit as brokenhearted as Jude had felt only minutes earlier. "I wish I was, but he promised himself to her."

"Yeah, yeah, yeah," her father responded in annoyed voice.

The chapel seemed miles away. To Jude, the entire journey from St. Louis to Sacramento felt shorter than his dash to the other side of town.

Eventually, they reached the chapel. Jude paused for a moment, trying to force himself to accept and react appropriately to whatever fate awaited him on the other side of the door. He looked at the man who joined him in his task to interrupt the wedding, and they gave each other a slight nod of encouragement. Now was the time to fix things, if they still could be fixed.

Jude burst through the doors, the first to enter, and the man and his daughter stormed in behind him.

The preacher spoke in a loud voice, as though he were speaking to a full church and not one couple in front of the altar. "If anyone opposes this marriage, speak now or forever hold your peace."

"I oppose it," Jude boomed. He held a hand against his chest, trying to catch his breath. His heart was beating fast, more from fear that he was too late than exertion. He looked at Callie, who had a bouquet of lilies in her hands, a wreath of daisies around her head, and a stunned expression on her face. She looked at Jude with her wide green eyes. Jude broke into a huge smile. He could hardly believe his good fortune. Mesmerized by Callie's beauty and consumed by the knowledge that she had been only minutes away from being lost to him forever, he was only vaguely aware of the man from the saloon making his opposition known to the preacher too.

"This is highly unusual," the preacher muttered, looking as confused as Albert and Callie, and significantly less happy than either of them.

Jude walked down the aisle. He looked at Albert and said, "I love this woman, she loves me, and I'm going to be the one marrying her today."

With a stunned yet affable expression on his face, Albert stepped away and waved at Jude to take his place.

"Albert," Sara said softly, joining them along with her father in the front of the chapel. "I'm sorry about this."

"I'm not," Albert replied, flashing her a smile.

Callie was smiling now too. She placed her flowers on a pew and held both palms to her blushing cheeks. "You love me, Jude?"

He grinned at her and removed her hands from her face. He brought them to his lips and kissed each one. "I'm marrying you, aren't I?"

"I sure hope so," she said, and dissolved into delighted laughter.

Jude turned to the preacher. "Reckon you can finish what you started, only use Jude Johnson for the name of the groom?"

The preacher threw up his hands. "Why not?"

And so Callie and Jude got married, followed immediately by Albert and Sara. The four of them visited with each other after the unusual and happy turn of events. Jude had a feeling that they would all become very good friends if he and Callie settled in Sacramento. He could already imagine their children playing together.

"It was her outlandish stories that first got me curious," Jude explained to the other couple. He gave Callie a stern look. "And I still intend to find out which of her stories are true and which are false."

Albert laughed. "Like how she attended opera every Friday night in St. Louis?"

Jude sighed. "That's a new one to me."

Callie peered at Jude sheepishly through her

lashes and giggled.

"Think it's funny, do you?" Jude said with mock severity. "We'll see how funny it is when you're lying face-down over my lap."

Callie stopped giggling but her eyes still sparkled. She looked happier than Jude had ever seen her. He was eager to get on to the next part of the evening, so he took their leave and grabbed Callie's hand. "Come along, wife."

Callie let out a gleeful squeak. "Right away, *husband*."

CHAPTER ELEVEN

Jude removed each pin that connected the wreath of flowers to her hair. "You look so beautiful, Callie," he said, as he lifted the wreath from her head. He placed it on the table and then folded her into his embrace. "This went from being the saddest day of my life to being the happiest."

She circled her arms around his neck and gazed up at him. "I feel the same. I've never been so happy as I am right now, Jude. I loved you, but I wanted to be a good person and follow through on my promise to Albert."

"I know, honey. Such a good girl." He bent and brushed her lips with his. When she moaned and leaned into him, he captured her mouth and took what was now rightfully his. He set about exploring her sweet mouth. He'd wanted to kiss her for what seemed like ages, and it felt like heaven to finally be able to do so. He pulled away, leaving her panting and her swollen lips parted. She let out a soft whimper of protest.

"We have some business to attend to, darlin'." He reached around her and unfastened the first of her crystal buttons, then undid each one down to the delicate dip of her back. He peeled the sleeves from her arms, revealing her thin chemise, which couldn't hide her peaked nipples.

He dropped the dress slowly down over her hips. "Step out, my love," he instructed when the dress pooled around her feet on the floor.

She did as she was told, balancing by placing her hands on his shoulders. "Are you going to make love to me, Jude?"

"Why, yes, I am, darlin'." He slowly pulled her chemise over her head and took in the sight of her swollen breasts. He cupped one in his hand and caressed her nipple with his thumb, while his other hand lingered on her back. "But first, we're going to play a game."

Her eyes half-lidded and hazy with desire, she said breathlessly, "Game?"

"Mm hmm." He bent and kissed her again before he walked to the small desk in the corner, picked up the straight-back chair, and returned to where she stood. After planting the chair beside her, he sat down and patted his legs with both hands. "Over you go."

Her lips formed into a pout immediately. "I don't like this game."

"You don't know that, you haven't played it yet. Come on now, lickety-split." He took her arm and guided her across his lap.

She landed and shifted over his legs. She was wearing lacy drawers that matched her new dress. He admired them briefly before he looped his finger under the ribbon tying them around her waist and tugged the fabric down the length of her legs, removing them completely. She squealed when he placed his hand on her bare bottom.

"What's the name of this game?" she squeaked.

Jude kneaded her plump little cheeks, finding great pleasure in seeing and touching her bare bottom for the first time. "It's called 'Truth or Spank.'"

Callie giggled, and Jude couldn't help but chuckle as well. He pulled off each of her shoes and rolled her stockings down her calves and off her feet. He took in the sight of his beautiful, fully naked wife lying over his lap, the picture of innocence, vulnerability, and arousal. His cock hardened and he cleared his throat. "Do you want to know the rules of the game?"

"I guess," she grumbled.

Jude brought his hand down smartly on her right cheek. "First rule is respect. Care to change your response?" He smacked her left cheek.

"Yes, please! I want to know the rules," she amended, and squirmed.

"Better." He rubbed the sting out of the places where he'd just smacked. "The rules are simple. I'm going to ask you some questions, and you're going to answer. For each lie, you get punished, but for each truth you get rewarded. Are you ready?"

She shifted again. "May I ask a question first?"

"Of course, darlin'."

"I know what the punishment is, but... what's the reward?"

"That's a good question, baby." He wrapped his hand around her thigh and gently pulled her leg to him, revealing her sex to his view. She already glistened with desire. He slid his hand to her womanhood and dipped a finger between her folds. He tickled her nub, causing her to gasp and open her legs wider to him. He gave her clit one final flick before removing his hand from her center.

"The rewards will be similar to that," he told her. He patted her bottom firmly. "Let's get started. First, I know you lied about your whipping skills the day that we met, so that's five swats."

"But Jude, you already punished—"

He brought his hand down. *Smack*. "Doesn't matter. I make up the rules of this game." He landed four more moderate swats on the low curve of her bottom, just barely hard enough to leave a sting for him to caress out of her cheeks.

She let out a noise that sounded somewhere between a growl and a moan and grasped his trouser leg with her fist.

"Next question. Did you really study under the tutelage of Florence Nightingale? Keep in mind when you answer that I am aware she lives across the ocean."

Callie wriggled over his lap, which Jude thought looked quite adorable but which caused his cock a fair bit of discomfort as her belly rubbed against him. "Not exactly," she admitted. "I did learn some nursing from someone who read her book, and I—"

"Bad girl," he interrupted in a growl, and smacked her thighs lightly, twice on each side, then landed a good hard smack on her bottom.

"Ooooh, that stings!" She reached back and rubbed her bottom furiously.

"*Tsk tsk*, move that hand, young lady. Your naughty bottom is all mine tonight. You're not allowed to touch what's mine without permission."

He watched her body shudder with embarrassment and arousal. When she removed her hand, he landed a swat where she'd touched and grabbed hold. "Mine," he repeated in a low voice. She moaned and arched her back.

Rubbing the spot he'd just spanked, he said, "Time for a little reward." His fingers traveled to between her legs. "Mmm. You're soaked, darlin'. Someone is enjoying her spanking." He rolled his finger around her pleasure nub and gave it a pinch, then brushed back and forth over it. "This is for the truth about Jesse James teaching you how to shoot," he explained. His voice was thick with desire, as was his manhood.

She let out little whimpers and gasps and pressed into his hand, searching for her release.

"This is mine too," he growled, cupping her sex possessively. "I decide when you get pleasure. I decide when you get punished."

"Oh, Jude, I ache. Please keep rubbing," she begged in a whimper.

"No, I think that's enough pleasure for now. Next question," he stated, his hand remaining still on her womanhood. "Do you really know how to fix all the parts on a stagecoach?"

She crossed and uncrossed her ankles in the air, nervous and jittery with erotic energy. "Sam let me help him and his boy fix up a broken-down buggy. I reckon lots of the parts are the same as on a coach, so maybe I know how to fix about half of them."

Jude grinned. "Then I reckon that's two spanks, two pleasure rubs, and one that's a little of both." He brought his hand back and smacked her quivering, naked bottom, then grinned even more as she lifted her bottom to meet his hand for the next swat. "Good girl," he murmured, and gave her a sound spank. He dragged his fingers through her wetness and rubbed her clit until she writhed in his hand. "Now for the half-pleasure, half-punishment," he rumbled. "Open your legs wide for me, baby."

She didn't hesitate. She was dripping wet, her whole body trembling with desire. Jude patted her sex a couple times, then drew his hand away and landed it in a hard smack directly on her mound and sensitive clit. She screamed, pleasure and pain melding into one shattering release.

"That's it," he said huskily. He wrapped a hand around her hip and held her steady while lightly stroking her sex with his other hand until she settled.

She hung over his lap, breathing hard while he caressed her from her shoulders to her freshly spanked bottom.

"How'd you end up liking that game?"

"I liked it a lot," she said softly.

"Good girl. You deserve more pleasure for telling the truth about that." He lifted her into his arms and settled her on the bed. She watched him as he stripped. When he loosened his belt and let his trousers drop, the evidence of his arousal displayed prominently, its head wet with a trickle of his seed.

* * *

Callie stared at his cock with a mixture of curiosity and apprehension. She'd never seen a man's member before, although she knew the particulars of sex. "Are you going to shove that into me now?"

He laughed and climbed over her, straddling her hips with his knees. "I'd like to think of it as a polite entrance, but actually your description is probably more apt on this occasion."

She wrapped her arms around his neck as he bent to kiss her. His kiss traveled from her lips to her jaw down her neck to her breast. He swirled around her nipple with his tongue. With his knee, he spread her legs, allowing him access to her drenched channel. Callie felt her womb constrict and her desire grow as he arranged her for his pleasure.

"Remind me whose this is," he growled in her ear as he penetrated her entrance with the tip of his cock.

"Yours," she moaned.

"Mm hmm, that's right." He pressed in a little farther, and Callie felt a wave of panic. He was too big, she felt too full.

"It hurts," she whimpered, pressing her bottom into the bed in an attempt to free herself from the beginning of his impalement. She squeezed her eyes shut.

He held her hips in his hands firmly to prevent her from detaching herself but stopped moving forward. "I hear it hurts women the first time, honey. Not much I can do about that, but the pain won't last."

She opened her eyes and stared into his, which regarded her with intense lust but also a glimmer of kindness she knew and trusted. "Promise?" she whispered.

He reached up and stroked a stray lock of hair away from her forehead with a slow finger.

"I promise. I imagine it's kinda like that spanking I just gave you. Hurts some but then the pleasure makes it worth it in the end."

"All right, Jude," she said in a moan. Her heart fluttered wildly. She felt afraid, curious, and even more aroused after his reassurance.

He kissed her neck. "Take a deep breath and relax, honey."

She drew in a breath, and as she released it, she forced her taut muscles to loosen. That's when he speared her, plunging into her with the full length of his cock. She screamed from the sharp pain and tears sprang to her eyes. She felt desperate to get away from the offending member that, even as the pain subsided, still stretched the walls of her center to an uncomfortable width. She wriggled her hips, but Jude held fast to them and remained fully engorged inside of her.

"Stop moving. Relax and breathe," she heard Jude say, and she became aware that she was holding her breath. She let it out. She continued to breathe deeply, staring into Jude's eyes. His cock still felt uncomfortably big inside of her, but she realized she was experiencing a new kind of discomfort. She desperately needed his cock to stroke and caress her channel. Her muscles constricted with need.

His jaw clenched. He looked uncomfortable too, and he spoke through gritted teeth. "You feel so warm, so tight. I need to move, darlin'."

She nodded at him and then felt the first

blissful stroke. She moaned as his length glided through her passage, sparking to life every nerve of her body.

"God, you feel good," he said, and sped up his thrusts.

"You feel good too." She no longer shied away from his movements but rose to meet him each time he rocked toward her.

Her pleasure built until she crested again, moaning out her release as she dug her fingers into his back. He came just after, groaning along with her moan, and released his seed deep inside of her.

They lay panting and entangled in each other's arms. She sighed contentedly and played with the sparse dark hair on his chest, while he languidly ran his fingers through her hair and down her back.

When she found her voice, she asked, "Can we live in Sacramento, Jude? I love it here."

"Yes."

She giggled. "That was easy. I must remember to always ask you for things right after lovemaking."

He smiled. "I was actually going to suggest it. I've saved enough to buy a house and some land. I want to get into ranching."

"No more driving?"

He shook his head. "It's not a good job for a married man. I wouldn't mind doing it maybe once a year or so for some extra tin, though."

"Can I come with you? I can be the guard

and sit with you up front. After all, I was taught to shoot by Jesse James," she said playfully.

Jude ran a hand down her arm, marveling at how soft her skin felt. "You just reminded me of another lie I need to spank you for."

She frowned and lifted her head to look at him. "What?"

"You claimed at the start of the journey that you'd be no trouble whatsoever and I'd hardly notice you were there. I do believe you made your presence quite well known every minute of every day for the entire trip."

Her frown turned into a smile. "I'm real sorry about that, Jude."

He cuddled her against his chest and wrapped his arms around her. "You are not," he whispered, and kissed her cheek. "And that's another lie."

She sighed with contentment in his arms, knowing she was safe, loved, and exactly where she belonged. She fell into a peaceful sleep.

* * *

One year later

Jude downed his whiskey and set the tumbler on the bar of Sacramento's busiest saloon. "I'll be back in about two months. I'm mighty obliged to you, offering to check from time to time into how my foreman's doing at the ranch."

Albert took a much more gentlemanly sip of his liquor and swirled the remainder around in his glass. "It's my pleasure. I hope your journey east and back goes by fast for you."

Jude stood from the stool and donned his Stetson. "It'll fly by in a jiffy. Traveling the line for two months a year is just right. It takes financial pressure off running the ranch and gives me and Callie more time to sit back and enjoy it."

Albert nodded his understanding. "Say hi to my catalog bride for me and give her a good smack for lying in her letters about knowing how to ride. I saw her trying to mount a sweet ol' mare yesterday. I'm not sure which of them was more confused about what she was aiming to do."

Jude chuckled. "I'll give her your regards. And give my best to Sara, along with a big kiss for garnering your affection. I don't believe things could have worked out more perfectly for any of us."

"Have to agree with you there," Albert said with a grin.

Jude shook his friend's hand and exited the saloon. His stagecoach waited for him in the street, along with four ticketed passengers. He walked to them and made his introductions, then said, "I reckon I should give you a quick rundown of our journey, but I'm waiting for one more person to join us."

"I'm here," a voice behind him said. He

turned and grinned at Callie as she strutted to his side. She wore a faded blue dress, sturdy new boots, and a revolver at her hip.

Jude snaked his arm around her waist and introduced her to the passengers. "This here is my guard. She gets the box seat because she's a darn good shot and will keep us all safe on our journey."

Callie smiled and said hello to everyone. When the last of the horses was checked and the groom bade them farewell, Jude, Callie, and the passengers climbed into their respective seats on the coach.

Jude cracked his whip and urged the horses into a smart walk, then looked over at his wife, hardly believing it was the same girl who'd joined him in the box seat all those months ago. She looked calmer, happier, and a fair bit cleaner than the first time he laid eyes on her.

Still, the girl he first fell in love with wasn't far beneath the surface. She turned her mischievous green eyes to him. "This trip, I promise I won't be as much trouble to you."

He raised an eyebrow. "Not sure how impressive a promise that is. If we make it to the first stop without any shenanigans, you will have improved over last time."

Callie patted her new satchel that she'd placed between them on the seat. "There won't be any need to stop for gingerroot this time. I found some beforehand and packed it."

Jude nodded in appreciation. "Well now,

that's right smart thinking, darlin'." He steered his horses around a bend and peered into the distance. He felt a surge of gratitude for the direction his life had taken. The road stretched ahead of them as far as he could see, with no end in sight, and he couldn't have felt happier about the journey they were on together.

The End

BOOKS IN THIS SERIES

Cowboys in Charge

Caught By The Lawman

A scared young woman accused of theft stands in front of Marshal Jake Huntley's desk at the jailhouse. The lawman generally has no tolerance for criminals, but when she focuses her doleful blue eyes on him in a way that makes his heart race, he wants nothing more than to protect her.

Elizabeth Matthews is in desperate need of help, but she refuses to tell the truth when the marshal demands it. It's his job to protect people, but it's also his job to punish criminals, so how can she?

Though the lawman doesn't plan to use the law against her, he's not opposed to delivering justice in the form of a hard, bare-bottomed spanking over his knee. After her bottom is thrashed to a deep shade of crimson, her secrets spill out. Will the marshal be able to save her from enemies on both sides of the law?

Her Gruff Boss

The man Anna Brown comes to work for is not the amiable man she once knew. This version of Carter Barnes is gruff, impatient, and seems to be doing his best to ignore Anna's very existence.

And she's not putting up with it for one second longer.

An uncharacteristic display of temper from Anna seems to shock Carter out of his apathy, much to her delight. Even his discipline, which leaves her bottom red and burning, excites her in ways she's never known.

But a villain's vicious attack shatters Anna's newfound happiness, and the fallout sends her fleeing from the home. When Carter follows, she's forced to decide whether to trust him with her heart and return to the life they've built together...

Or turn her back for good on the only man she's ever loved.

A Vexing Woman

As soon as she steps off the train into the hot

southwestern sun, Charlotte Rose wonders if she has made a mistake. Leaving Boston to take a job as the schoolmarm of the small town of Porter, Texas, had seemed like a good idea, but the man sent to fetch her from the station almost changes her mind.

The handsome but uncivilized brute who introduces himself as Max Harrison not only calls Charlotte by her first name, he also demands that she change her clothing, which he insists is inappropriate for the weather.

She refuses to obey him. A short time later she gets heatstroke, faints, and endures being undressed down to her unmentionables and splashed with water by the brute. Worse, after her humiliating experience, Max warns her that any further foolishness will earn her a sound spanking on her bare bottom.

Somehow, despite his threat to chastise her in such a barbaric fashion, being in Max's presence sets Charlotte's heart fluttering. And when confronted by the dangers of the new town, he might be the only man she can trust.

His Little Saloon Girl

Lily has dreamed of performing on stage since she was a small child, and at the age of eighteen she approaches Jesse, the owner of the local saloon, to ask for a job singing and dancing for his customers.

Jesse refuses to hire her, insisting that the saloon is no place for a sweet, innocent girl like Lily. When she persists in her request, he pulls her over his knee for a hard spanking followed by a stern warning never to set foot in the saloon again.

Now she not only wants Jesse to hire her, she also wants to call him Daddy.

Will Lily ever convince Daddy to let her be his little saloon girl, or will the spankings continue until she learns that Daddy will do whatever it takes to protect her?

Bringing Trouble Home

Widowed rancher Heath Wolfe worries he's making a big mistake by bringing Willow McAllister home to his ranch. A known troublemaker around town, she can't seem to keep a job or avoid skirmishes with the law, so the town marshal implores Heath to help. While Heath agrees to employ Willow, he certainly won't allow misbehavior, and he's even prepared to take the willful young lady over his knee for a sound spanking if warranted.

Orphaned and alone for several years, nineteen-year-old Willow is used to taking care of herself. She sleeps wherever she can find a soft surface and roams freely. She doesn't drink whiskey every night and she only steals when she has to, so it doesn't seem fair when the marshal insists she give up her freedom to work for Heath. She suspects that the rancher is as humorless as he is handsome.

Heath and Willow are as different as two people can be, but a tentative friendship forms. Old habits die hard, though, and it doesn't take long for Willow to engage in familiar shenanigans. When problems arise, will Heath regret bringing trouble home, or has Willow finally found a man who can steer her straight?

When He Returns

Proud and independent, thirteen-year-old orphan Wade Hunter doesn't want a family. But when the town marshal catches him stealing, Wade's given only two choices: Spend time in jail or become the marshal's ward.

Sadie Shaw, the marshal's eldest daughter, doesn't want another sibling. She has enough brothers and sisters, and she's dismayed when her kindhearted pa brings home another lost child. It doesn't help that this one is surly and arrogant.

Worse, he thinks that because he's older, he's under no obligation to mind her household rules.

Wade and Sadie battle wills often as they grow into adulthood, burgeoning both their dislike for each other and their grudging respect. When faced with a problem that requires their unity, will they be able to set aside their differences, or will the strife they face only tear them apart for good?

Taming Tori

Roughhewn cowboy Frank Bassett knows his life has changed forever after a near-fatal horse accident leaves him with a serious limp. Determined to make the best of his circumstances, he takes a job as a schoolteacher in a small town. There he crosses paths with a beautiful, tart-tongued seamstress, who before long finds herself over his knee to be taught a richly deserved lesson in good manners.

Frank does not fit the bill with regard to Victoria Davis's hope of landing herself a wealthy husband, but the snobby young woman can't resist the magnetic pull of Frank's strength, dominance, and tenderness. She becomes hopelessly smitten, and a tempestuous romance ignites.

But dark clouds loom ahead, and a stroke of misfortune will once again befall the cowboy. Can these two spirited lovers weather the impending storm, or will their love be collateral damage?

Mary Quite Contrary

Nineteen-year-old Mary Appleton manages a successful restaurant in the small town of Thorndale. Though passionate about cooking, she's naïve about the dangers of the world and innocent when it comes to love and romance.

Benjamin Gray, the stern new deputy in town, knows the restaurant is vulnerable to robbers, and his protective instincts ignite when he notices that Mary doesn't safeguard her money. When she refuses to lock up the cash in her register, Deputy Gray gives her only one other choice: Accept a hard spanking over his knee.

To Mary's surprise, the punishment does nothing to quell her attraction to Ben. Rather, she finds herself smitten by her older lover who brings her as much pleasure as pain. But will she accept his advice when it matters most, or will her contrary behavior ruin them both?

Trapped With The Mountain Man

Times are hard in Montana in the mid-1800s, and when Nettie finds herself impoverished, desperate, and alone after the death of her husband, she flees the town of Helena to escape the clutches of the local saloon owner. But living off the land quickly proves much more difficult than she'd hoped, and after days without food she resorts to stealing from Jack Abrams, a gruff mountain man and trapper who lives a secluded, uncomplicated life in the woods.

Jack doesn't take kindly to being stolen from and when he catches her red-handed, Nettie ends up lying naked over his knee for a long, hard spanking. To her surprise, however, after her punishment Jack offers her food and shelter in return for cooking, cleaning, and doing as she is told. But Nettie is determined to never rely on a man again, and with a belly full of food and renewed determination, she abandons him to take another shot at living in the woods on her own.

Jack knows the headstrong girl won't survive without his help, especially when she chooses a grizzly's winter cave as her shelter, and he can't stand by and idly watch her demise. When his irritation with her foolish pride boils over, he decides it is time to show her how thoroughly a man can dominate a woman silly enough to venture into the woods alone. Jack's stern chastisement and bold mastery of her body leave Nettie begging for more, but is she truly ready to give up her freedom to be claimed by the mountain man?

Made in the USA
Las Vegas, NV
21 October 2023

79494361R00095